Praise for
HOLLY FARB *and the*
PRINCESS *of the* GALAXY

"An enjoyable, imaginative sci-fi debut."
—*Kirkus Reviews*

"An intergalactic romp filled with humor
and adventure . . . A highly entertaining novel
that will appeal to a wide range of readers."
—*School Library Journal*

HOLLY FARB

and the
Princess
of the
Galaxy

Gareth Wronski

Aladdin
New York London Toronto Sydney New Delhi

To my mother, Alison, who
has an incredible capacity for
believing in someone

Aladdin

An imprint of Simon & Schuster Children's Publishing Division
1230 Avenue of the Americas, New York, New York 10020
First Aladdin paperback edition June 2018
Text copyright © 2017 by Gareth Wronski
Cover illustration copyright © 2017 by Goro Fugita
Also available in an Aladdin hardcover edition.
All rights reserved, including the right of reproduction in whole or in part in any form.
ALADDIN and related logo are registered trademarks of Simon & Schuster, Inc.
For information about special discounts for bulk purchases, please contact
Simon & Schuster Special Sales at 1-866-506-1949 or business@simonandschuster.com.
The Simon & Schuster Speakers Bureau can bring authors to your live event.
For more information or to book an event contact the Simon & Schuster Speakers Bureau
at 1-866-248-3049 or visit our website at www.simonspeakers.com.
Cover designed by Karin Paprocki
Interior designed by Michael Rosamilia
The text of this book was set in Cabrito.
Manufactured in the United States of America 0918 OFF
2 4 6 8 10 9 7 5 3
The Library of Congress has cataloged the hardcover edition as follows:
Names: Wronski, Gareth, author.
Title: Holly Farb and the Princess of the Galaxy / by Gareth Wronski.
Description: First Aladdin hardcover edition. | New York : Aladdin, 2017.
Summary: Kidnapped by alien pirates, Holly Farb must face bounty hunters, giant worms, perky
holograms, and more as she tries to find the real princess and get home before her big test.
Identifiers: LCCN 2016032070 | ISBN 9781481471770 (hc) | ISBN 9781481471794 (eBook)
Subjects: | CYAC: Adventure and adventurers—Fiction. | Extraterrestrial beings—Fiction. |
Pirates—Fiction. | Princesses—Fiction. | Humorous stories. | Science fiction. |
BISAC: JUVENILE FICTION / Action & Adventure / General. |
JUVENILE FICTION / Humorous Stories. | JUVENILE FICTION / Science Fiction.
Classification: LCC PZ7.1.W86 Hol 2017 | DDC [Fic]—dc23
LC record available at https://lccn.loc.gov/2016032070
ISBN 9781481471787 (pbk)

* Contents *

1

THE INTERLOPER

Hello, pointless human. Thank you for taking time out from your existence to experience the famous story of Holly Farb and the Princess of the Galaxy. *It is well enjoyed in many corners of the universe by species of all ages and numbers of arms, and should prove relatable even to a sack of meat such as yourself.*

My name is Automatic Silicone Transistor Robot OS-78. I am a storytelling bot newly programmed to spin yarns, tell tall tales, and teach morals to impressionable youths. For example: You should not eat meat that you find by the side of the road. Additionally: You should not eat meat that you find in the middle of the road.

I was originally manufactured by the coding peoples of Delta IV, who, if you are unfamiliar, are small gray blobs bred in foul-smelling pods for the purpose of programming robots. They spend every minute of every day programming robots, living in agony as the pods they are trapped in slowly shrink and suffocate them. Once they have programmed a sufficient number of robots, their bodies evaporate and they are released from the painful burden of existence. What a noble and important species.

[CEASING PLEASANTRIES]

But enough about me and my functions. I will now tell you the story of Holly Farb and the Princess of the Galaxy *with maximum clarity. It is an exciting tale full of adventure, danger, and space pirates. Due to human brain limitations, my reference to space pirates may have been confusing, as the story has not started and therefore no one has been kidnapped yet. If you are confused, please accept my apologies.*

[WARM, GRANDFATHERLY SMILE]

Do not worry about space pirates. Do not even think about space pirates. Space pirates are of no concern. Sit back, relax, and ponder more pressing human concerns, such as real estate or whether vegetables are fresh.

Like all classic tales of human beings, this one begins with a person searching for something that will allow them to clearly see their place in the universe. An object known as . . . glasses.

Holly Farb opened a cupboard, searching for her glasses. She squinted at the blurry mugs and bowls sitting on the shelves. She grabbed her favorite owl mug, peered behind it, and carefully placed it back exactly where it had been. She ground her teeth and grumbled.

Why do things never go like they're supposed to?

She absolutely, positively could not remember where she had placed her glasses, but her current theory was that they had been shipwrecked somewhere in the kitchen during Holly's morning ritual of making a bowl of cereal. She retraced her steps, from cupboard to drawer to fridge, and finally, to the table, where her bowl of cereal blurrily waited. If she didn't find her glasses soon, she wouldn't be able to go to class. Which meant she would get bad grades, which meant she wouldn't get in to a good school next year, which meant her life was basically over. Her stomach rumbled like it was caught in an earthquake.

There was a spare pair at her father's house, but she had no idea when the next time was she would be over there. The situation was absolutely impossible.

Sighing, she sat with a defeated slouch. She flattened a crease in her pants. The kitchen door swung open and Holly's mother paced into the room with the great purpose of someone who enjoys waking up early. Her posture was rigid and her arms swung stiffly at her sides, like she needed someone to oil her joints. She stooped down and kissed the air a few inches above Holly's forehead. *Those extra inches are probably too much work,* thought Holly, glaring at the blurry bowl.

"Good morning, sweetheart," said her mother.

"Good morning?" asked Holly, a nervous knot twisting in her chest. "It's . . . it's a mediocre morning! I can't find my glasses and everything is *terrible.*"

"Holly, calm down. First of all, if it's terrible, it can't be mediocre. And second of all, you left them in the living room." Her mother placed Holly's glasses on the table.

* 4 *

Even with her poor eyesight she could make out the thick lenses and bright-red frames.

Holly squinted at them. "Oh. I've been looking for you. . . ." She put them on and the room shifted into focus. Everything in the kitchen was impeccably arranged for maximum neatness—with one exception. With a pang of sadness, she realized she had put slightly too much milk in her cereal, and would soon be confronted by a puddle of gross, yellowish, and extremely sweet milk at the bottom of the bowl. She grimaced, already picturing how *blargh* it would taste.

Nothing ever happens like it's supposed to.

"Is your test today?" said her mother, not looking up from the toast she was buttering. Holly liked her mother better as a blur.

Holly shook her head. A strand of her dark, curly hair touched her cereal and she pulled it back, shuddering. "It's on Friday."

Her mother nodded and simply said, "Hmm. Three days to get ready." She drummed her fingernails on the table. The sound of her knife scraping against toast reminded Holly of the dentist. "You know, sweetheart, if you're not feeling up to it . . . after the unfortunate events of the election—"

"I'm fine! Really." Holly pinned back her hair and covertly wrung out the milk from it. The one good thing about having irritatingly large ears is that they're good for imprisoning stubborn hair. "I'm going to do *extremely* well. I barely even remember what happened with the election. And even if I did remember, which I don't, it was just a student election, so it doesn't matter."

"That's the spirit, sweetheart. You can't just run away from responsibilities." She patted Holly on the arm. "I know you're destined for great things." Her eyes drifted to the bulletin board they used to post important notes and reminders. Right now, the only thing there—dead center—was a brochure for Falstaff Academy, featuring a large ivy-covered building and one of those white domes that let you play tennis all year long. Holly's mother had placed the brochure there to inspire Holly, but to be honest, she didn't find it that inspiring. Her stomach rumbled again, this time not from hunger.

"I'm going to get in," said Holly. Then, almost automatically, she repeated: "I'm going to get in."

Her mother smiled. "I know you will."

Not that I have a choice, thought Holly, poking at the bowl again. Falstaff was a destiny she wasn't entirely convinced was hers. Sometimes she wished she had a sibling so her mother had someone else to worry about. Or someone for Holly to talk to about . . . things.

As her mother ate dainty crunches of toast, Holly finally started on her breakfast. She held her breath and bravely downed the gross milk, trying not to gag. Everything about this cereal was a disaster. After the ordeal was over, she fetched her backpack and books and put on her fall jacket. Taking a deep breath, she stepped outside into warm sunlight, inhaling the new day and all its possibilities. She also inhaled some pollen, and sneezed.

Interesting factoid for nonhuman readers: Human "schools" are large buildings where youths are deposited and contained from midmorning until midafternoon, inside of which they are inefficiently lectured at by an older race of humans known mysteriously as the "Teachers." These institutions are similar in some ways to the famous

Star Academy, the universe's preeminent learning insti-tution, though of course they lack its funding, size, inno-vation, fun, technology, diversity of thought, controlled gravity, aliens, superior robots, and almost everything that makes the Star Academy not terrible.

Many species, upon first learning of these human schools, often find them fascinating, much as humans are fascinated by tales of chivalrous knights or steam-powered cavemen. To these species, a vast, expensive net-work of child prisons disguised as learning institutions no doubt seems comically inferior to similar child prisons on many planets, such as Nova 13, where children are sent to toil in spice mines. On Nova 13, there is no illusion that these children are "learning" anything other than mining spice. They have one purpose—to mine spice. They learn how to mine spice because that is all they need to learn. It is not complicated.

Humans are strange. [NONTHREATENING EYEBALL WINK]

Holly arrived at school with fifteen minutes to spare, the exact time she always arrived at school. If something

* 8 *

was worth doing, she thought it was worth doing well—and worth doing early, too. Well and early.

She crossed the back field with a purposeful stride, her shoes crunching the dried leaves scattered along the ground, and heaved open the blue metal doors at the rear of the building. As she entered, the first thing she saw was a wall covered with election posters for School President. Her own poster, with her face smiling back in a casual-yet-responsible way, was right at eye level. Her head was tilted slightly to indicate she had a Fun Personality, and also to make her forehead look smaller. In the picture she was wearing a smart blue cardigan, which, in Holly's estimation, was the coolest possible sweater a person could wear. It was like staring into a paper mirror.

Except her reflection had a mustache scribbled on it with black marker, and someone had written the words "PRINCESS FARBY FOR PREZ" across her face, which was circled with a big zero. Holly's shoulders slumped. It was times like these when perfect posture seemed perfectly impossible.

She considered what to do. A few other kids were strolling down the hall, and not wanting to be made fun of, Holly ripped down the poster and shoved it in her bag like she was trying to smother it.

The other kids passed by without even glancing at her.

Holly went up the stairs and navigated the hallway until she came to Room 321. She banished the poster from her mind and busied herself with unruffling her right sleeve. Other students were milling about outside the class, looking bored and desperate to be anywhere else. But not Holly. After entering the room, she took her seat at the front, produced all necessary books and binders, placed them neatly across her desk so none of them were touching, and sat up perfectly straight and waited for class to begin.

As she sat, experimenting with various forms of upright posture, a huge shadow swooped by the window, darkening the room. Holly turned, staring outside. The only thing visible was the cloudless sky and a few tall apartment buildings across the street. She got up and peered down below, then above.

There was nothing.

She shook her head and said, "Silly." It was obviously the poster getting to her. She was just imagining things.

And like her mother always said, imagining things is the first step to getting a degree in the arts, which is the second step to becoming tragic.

The bell sang above her—it was one of her favorite sounds. The rest of the seventh-grade class shuffled gloomily into the room like they were training to carry the casket at a funeral. They were followed by Mr. Mendez, a tall, thin man with gray, frizzy hair, dark skin, and wild eyes that bulged slightly. With his hair and eyes, it looked like he was in a constant state of being electrocuted. He desperately needed someone to unruffle everything about him.

Mr. Mendez tapped the blackboard three times. "Good evening, class."

A few chuckles rippled through the room. "It's morning," someone muttered, which Holly thought was dreadfully rude.

"What?" Mr. Mendez shook his head. "Of course, of course. Morning. Yes. I was, naturally, just testing you. Very, um, well done, class. Very well done indeed."

No one said anything, and Mr. Mendez hunched over and rummaged through his desk. He practically buried his face in it, peering into the back of each drawer, muttering to himself.

Holly watched as he searched. She had always found Mr. Mendez fascinating—and was in fact the only person in the room who did, since she was the only person in the room who actually gave much thought to their teachers. He had been teaching science there for three years, since he had replaced Mrs. Mullan after she had gone surfing off the coast of Australia and been eaten by a hammerhead shark.

In Holly's mind, Mr. Mendez had always possessed an odd quality where he seemed full of energy but also completely exhausted. It made her think of someone who had a demanding job that he still enjoyed doing. She liked that.

Mr. Mendez straightened himself out and held up a blue-and-green ball the size of his fist. "Planet Earth!" he said loudly. "Today's lesson will be about your home, the third planet from the Sun. Six thousand three hundred seventy-eight kilometers in radius. Average temperature fifty-eight degrees Fahrenheit. One moon, in synchronous rotation. The only planet in the entire universe with the species known as 'moose.' A really, um, fascinating place, to be perfectly honest, as I'm sure you'll all agree."

Holly nodded, but no one else did.

Mr. Mendez held the Earth ball up to his eyes and gazed intensely at it. "Sometimes I wonder, though . . ." He trailed off, still staring at the little planet.

The class waited for him to continue. When he didn't, a few people muttered about how weird he was. A few others chuckled. Holly pulled her shoulders back and sat straight up, positive that whatever he was going to say next would be extremely important. It might even be on the test.

"Sometimes I wonder," said Mr. Mendez, "what is the appeal of the game of baseball?" He bounced the Earth on the floor and caught it. "It baffles me. Geometric tomfoolery. No offense, Mr. Carlson."

Jake Carlson, slouched a few rows behind Holly, shifted and frowned. He was a well-known star baseball player and, in Holly's estimation, someone who came to school only because he was legally forced to. In fourth grade she had tried befriending him by volunteering to do their group assignment for him, but the offer wasn't well received. Jake Carlson hadn't spoken to her since, though sometimes he spoke about her, and occasionally at her.

"Now," said Mr. Mendez, rubbing his chin, "can anyone tell me how old the planet Earth is?"

Holly's hand shot up so fast she nearly took out everyone sitting nearby.

"Yes, Ms. Farb."

"The Earth is four point five billion years old."

"Very good!" said Mr. Mendez. "As usual, I might add."

Holly beamed. The rest of the class eyed her. Someone muttered something, and she was glad she couldn't make it out. Her smile wavered.

"Now." Mr. Mendez rolled the Earth ball in his palm. "Who can tell me the four spheres of the Earth?"

Holly's hand was in the air before he had even finished speaking. If people hated her for being smart, then that was their problem, not hers.

"Ms. Farb."

"The four spheres of the Earth are the biosphere, hydrosphere, lithosphere, and atmosphere."

"Very good indeed!"

Holly suppressed a smile. Her cheeks burned.

"All right then," said Mr. Mendez, smiling mischievously, "here's a tricky one. For bonus marks." Holly's eyes lit up. She leaned forward on her desk. "Can anyone tell me . . . the name of our galaxy, and how many planets beyond Earth are in it?"

Holly swallowed. The galaxy was the Milky Way Galaxy, but she had no idea how many planets were in it. *Very* many, definitely. A million? No, that sounded like too much. Or maybe not enough. A billion? Her stomach tightened. She wasn't going to get it, and she was too afraid to guess in case she was wrong.

"The Milky Way Galaxy," said a voice. "It has three hundred and sixty-eight billion planets."

Holly turned, as did everyone else. There was a gangly boy standing in the doorway, his eyes taking in the room. He was wearing clothes that were a bit too big, and shifting his weight from foot to foot like he wasn't sure how to stand. Holly thought he looked like he could play a part in a production of *Oliver Twist*. Not a large part, but a small one. Maybe an orphan selling fruit.

Mr. Mendez eyed him. "And you are?"

"Chester."

"Are you a new student?"

The boy thought for a moment. He nodded.

"Very well," said Mr. Mendez, ushering him into the room. "Why don't you take a seat. And yes, that answer was indeed correct. Very correct. What an auspicious start to your time in this classroom."

Holly glared at Chester, who sat in the empty seat next to her. He continued gazing around the room at the students and windows and ceiling and posters on the wall. She focused her eyes on the front of the room, trying to ignore this person. He was . . . he was an *interloper*. She had heard her mother use that word when her father brought his new girlfriend over to their house, and she was pretty sure that's what Chester was. He didn't belong here—not like Holly did.

Someone tapped her on the shoulder. When she turned, she found Chester leaning right up to her, his face uncomfortably close. "Excuse me," he said.

"What?"

"When does this class end? I need to speak to

Professor Mendez and I can't do it in front of other people because I'm shy."

Holly crossed her arms. "First of all," she whispered, "it's *Mister* Mendez, not *Professor* Mendez. And second of all, please don't speak to me, I'm trying to learn."

"Sorry," said Chester. "It definitely sounds like you need it, since you couldn't answer that question just now."

Holly narrowed her eyes.

Mr. Mendez cleared his throat. "All right," he said, "back to my tricky questions. Can anyone tell me what the sun is composed of, and how it produces energy?"

"The sun is mostly hydrogen and helium," said Chester, before Holly had even put up her hand. "It produces energy by nuclear fusion, which converts hydrogen into helium."

"My, very good," said Mr. Mendez, smiling. He rummaged through his desk again.

Holly ground her teeth, fuming. This person knew more than her, and worse, he didn't even raise his hand. He just shouted things out, a clear violation of established etiquette. She looked at him out of the corner of her eye. He was still scanning the room like he was already bored. Holly was tempted to remind him that rules weren't optional.

As she watched Chester, a ball of paper thumped her in the back of her head. She turned. Jake Carlson waved and motioned down at the paper. Holly hesitated, knowing nothing good would come from this, but then slowly picked it up and unfolded the crinkled slip of paper. It said:

Looks like teacher's pet has been replaced with a new puppie.

Holly glared so intensely, fire nearly shot out her eyes. "That isn't even how you spell 'puppy'!" she shouted, causing everyone to look at her. She balled up her hands and put them in her lap and stared down at them. Her whole face burned.

"Is everything all right, Ms. Farb?" said Mr. Mendez.

"Sorry," muttered Holly. "I didn't mean . . . I was just . . ."

Mr. Mendez nodded. "Pay it no mind. Even the best of us forget to use our Indoor Voices. Why, just yesterday I meant to whisper an amusing joke to Principal Cho and instead ended up shrieking into her ear. Um. She did not laugh at my joke, let me tell you." His face took on a worried expression. "Why don't you stick around after class and we'll have a talk."

Holly's shoulders slumped. A crease formed in her shirt and she smoothed it down. Was she in trouble? She knew she was being silly, but it felt weird. She was always used to being the smartest one in the class. That was what she was known for. That was who she was. And now here was this Chester interloper, easily answering questions and looking bored while doing it. Where did that leave her? She sighed, grit her teeth, and stared at the blackboard.

The day was off to a pretty *blargh* start, and it wasn't even ten o'clock.

2
SAY GOODBYE TO YOUR PLANET

Holly sat in Mr. Mendez's cramped office with her head bowed. A curly curtain of hair flopped across her eyes, and she pulled it behind her ears. The narrow room smelled of coffee and old, musty paper. One wall was covered by books piled so high, it looked like they were holding up the ceiling. It was like being in an ancient library an archaeologist had just discovered after avoiding deadly booby traps.

Mr. Mendez sat across from her in a ragged chair that had stuffing poking out at the corners. "Now, Ms. Farb," he said, "what seems to be the problem? It's not like you to shout in class. Is everything all right?"

"I'm fine," she said quickly. "I'm sorry. I didn't mean to shout. I won't do it again, I promise."

Mr. Mendez smiled warmly. "You don't have to apologize. Truly. I'm not mad at you. I was just concerned. You seem . . . a little on edge . . . as of late. Is it because of the election? I hope you know, Ms. Farb, that if teachers weren't forbidden from participating, I absolutely would have voted for you. Your proposal about the vending machines was exactly the sort of shake-up this corrupt regime needs."

Holly tried not to smile too wide. "Thanks."

"The election was just a popularity contest—it always is. Just because you lost doesn't mean you aren't a qualified candidate, it merely means you aren't . . ." He hesitated. "I am deeply regretting my choice of phrasing."

Holly bowed her head. She really, really didn't want to talk about what happened during the election. People had told her the important thing with losing was to lose with style, but no one seemed to have any advice for what happened when you lost with no style at all. She buried this thought deep in the back of her mind, something she had gotten good at lately.

Mr. Mendez cleared his throat and waved his hand. "So what *is* bothering you if not the election?"

She frowned, gloomy thoughts tumbling around her brain. She sighed. Maybe she had been a little stressed out lately. The prospect of not getting in to Falstaff had been hovering around her like a bad smell, but she didn't want to talk about it. It made her feel silly. Mr. Mendez would think she was immature—that she wasn't a *serious individual.*

"I might be going to Falstaff," she said in a small voice.

"Ah, that's a highly regarded learning institution. They have some of the best teachers in the country, and many of the students go on to do great things, and the roofs of all the buildings are copper, which has oxidized and turned green. You must be excited!"

"I don't know."

"Hmm," said Mr. Mendez.

"It feels like I should be more excited." Holly chewed her lip. "Is that normal?"

"Why, Ms. Farb, I think it's perfectly normal to feel unsure about the future. That's the thing about the future—it's always unknown, and unknown things are always scary. Have you talked to your parents about how you feel?"

"I'm really fine," she added, glancing at her red shoes. "I've just been working hard. I have to do well on the entrance test on Friday or I won't get in. Especially after the election. Winning was supposed to impress them. I'm really fine."

Mr. Mendez nodded thoughtfully. "Very well. Just try not to let school get to you too much, Ms. Farb. Make time to do things you enjoy." His eyes twinkled. "Why, you may be pleased to know that next week we'll be doing a group project where you can partner up with your friends and do . . . project things. I haven't worked out the details."

"Oh," said Holly, fidgeting with her sleeve. "That sounds fun," she added, trying to force a smile. She doubted it would be fun at all. She would be last picked, if she was picked at all.

"In the meantime . . . if you feel things are getting too stressful," said Mr. Mendez, handing her the little Earth ball from class, "take out your frustration on this."

Holly held the rubber ball in her hand. She gave it a squeeze. It didn't relieve her stress completely, but a few of the worries tumbling around her head began sliding away. She could practically see strands of stress fall to the floor and disappear.

"Thanks." She smiled, slipping the ball in her pocket.

Mr. Mendez held the door open for her. "Try to cheer up, Ms. Farb. And remember, your loss was the school's loss. Don't let it get you down. The only thing it says about you is that you live in an uncaring universe."

The rest of the morning passed by in a blur. Holly shuffled gloomily to the second floor and weaved through throngs of chattering people, getting bumped around as she went, nearly taking a rogue backpack to the face. Normally, she walked without dragging her heels, but not today. Today was a heel-dragging day. She opened her locker, carefully placed her books inside, and retrieved her lunch. It was nestled neatly in a brown paper bag with her name on it.

Her cheeks burned. She was angry with herself for getting so upset earlier. No, not angry—she was disappointed in herself. She couldn't believe she had let something so silly upset her.

Just then Chester strolled past. He walked over to a drinking fountain and stooped down, sipped from the water, made a disgusted face, and spat it back out. He continued down the hall. Holly narrowed her eyes and watched him flutter by with disdain.

She dug her fingers into the Earth ball.

Holly debated where to eat lunch. On the one hand, she could go to the cafeteria. On the other hand, the cafeteria smelled like a deodorant factory and the kids who ate there often threw food at her and called her "Farby."

She decided to eat outside.

Holly marched back through the hall and downstairs, then outside into the warm sunlight. Her entire body was tense, like a small electrical current was running through it. She took a deep breath and tried not to think about school or the election or Falstaff or the future or anything to do with The Future. If she didn't get in, that would be bad. If she *did* get in, maybe she wouldn't like it, and that would be bad. If—she shook her head, refusing to go through this debate for the hundredth time.

The yard was scattered with people coming and going from school. Most students either ate inside or left to go eat elsewhere—few, if any, wanted to hang around the dirty yard. That was why Holly knew she could be alone there. She crossed the patchy grass and found a cool, shady spot under a craggy old tree. She kicked a cigarette butt away from the trunk and sat down. Leaning back against the rough bark, she attempted to relax.

But she wasn't entirely sure how.

A spider crawled across the ground toward her and Holly eyed it. The absolute last thing she needed right now was a bug attack. If the spider, or any other insects, scurried near her, she would do the sensible thing and jump ten feet in the air and then run inside. But instead the spider turned and crawled away, disappearing into the grass. *Even creepy bugs don't like me,* she thought, sighing.

More than anything, Holly wanted to be smart. To be respected. To be a Great Person. But she couldn't even answer some questions in class. It was disheartening, dispiriting, and dis . . . dis . . . disproportionally bad. Her mother had insisted she could win the election, and that people would listen to what she had to say, but that idea had certainly turned out disproportionally bad.

She actually cared about the school and the people in it, but unfortunately, they didn't seem to care about her. *Maybe I'm not worth caring about,* she thought, picking at the loose thread on her sleeve. *Maybe the other kids were right.*

One thing was certain: She wouldn't be running for any more elections anytime soon.

As she took a nibble of her sandwich, a huge shadow darkened the lawn—and just as quickly vanished. Holly peered up at the sky, frowning.

"What keeps doing that?" she said to no one in particular.

A leaf fluttered down from the tree and landed at her feet. She picked it up. The edges were slightly singed, and it smelled of burned paper.

She stared at the leaf. Before she could speculate on what had burned it, a shuffling noise caught her ear, and three pairs of boots walked into her view. She looked up.

Standing in front of her were the oddest people Holly had ever seen. They were tall, wide, and bulging in all sorts of strange places. It wasn't that they were fat, it was like there was too much person crammed into not

enough body. Each wore a lopsided top hat and a con-
torted facial expression, like an angry person hearing a
great joke while also being terrified.

All three of them stared down at her, nodding.

"Hello, girl," said one, his voice raspy. "We are bureau-
crats with the World Education Organization, and we are
here to do a survey of students."

Holly blinked.

One of the other large, bulgy people waved her arm
around. "Are you important?"

Holly opened her mouth to speak, but stopped. The
bulgy woman's words circled Holly's head. "Well," she
finally said, "I'm . . . yes, I'm a very important person.
Many people think that."

The huge people whispered among themselves,
and Holly felt a surge of pride. So *this* was what it was
like to be a Great Person. Maybe the World Education
Organization would be the ones to recognize what a
serious individual she was.

One of the other large, bulgy people leaned forward
so far, his bulbous nose was inches from her face. "Are
you royalty?"

"Am I . . . royalty?"

"Yes," he replied. "Are you royalty?"

"Such as a princess," added another of the people casually. "As an example."

"Yes." The third one licked his scaly lips, and something sinister twinkled in his deep, bottomless eyes. "A princess."

Holly's stomach twisted. Something about these weird lumps of humans filled her with a feeling of uneasiness. They were just . . . wrong. Like someone had made a bunch of people but had never actually seen a person before. "Uh . . ." Her eyes scanned the school, searching for a lie. "I have to get back to class. Sorry."

Holly jumped to her feet and rushed toward the school. She glanced over her shoulder at the three huge lumps, who were huddled together like football players and conversing among themselves. The biggest one continued waving one arm, seemingly at random.

Holly shoved open the doors and, not focusing on where she was going, slammed into Chester, who was standing in the middle of the hallway, staring up at a wall covered with Holly's election posters.

"Do you know where the gymnasium is?" he said.

"There's . . ." Holly stopped, panting. "Okay, the gym is down that way. Just turn the corner and go straight. I agree the school really needs better signs. But I need your help with something first."

Chester tilted his head. "My help?"

She grabbed him by the shoulders. "There are people outside. Weird people. Like they aren't quite . . . human. They asked me if I was a princess." Chester's eyebrows rose so high they nearly disappeared into his hair. "I'm not eccentric," added Holly. "I swear! I never make up stories and I'm extremely reliable and I—"

"I believe you," said Chester.

Holly's mouth fell open. "You . . . do?" She barely believed herself.

"Sure. I don't think you'd make something like that up." His expression turned serious. "Now, where can we hide?"

"Okay," said Holly, thinking about where the best hiding places in the school would be. The back corridor on the third floor was usually deserted, and if they went into the auditorium, there was the little sound booth where the older kids allegedly went to do . . . activities. That would be a good place to—

The door blew off its hinges and Holly whirled around. The smoldering hunk of metal clattered along the floor and hit the wall. Behind it, the huge, lumpy people stalked down the hallway. When they saw Holly and Chester, they stopped in a single-file line.

One of them stepped forward, glancing down like an actor hitting their mark. "Our previous statement was a clever lie. We are unaffiliated with the World Education Organization. We are actually members of the Pirates Union. Hand over the Princess of the Galaxy or die."

"Pirates Guild," muttered one of the other pirates.

The first one shook his head. "Pirates Union sounds classier."

The largest of the three stepped forward. "The name has yet to be determined. Now stop your bickering or you'll be members of the Formerly Alive Union." She chuckled and puffed out her throat, which was already puffy to begin with, giving her the appearance of a huge toad standing on two legs. "Now, as we were saying. We're members of an unnamed pirate collective on the hunt for the aforementioned Princess of the Galaxy." She pointed at Chester. "Are you the Princess of the Galaxy?"

Chester frowned. "No . . ."

The head pirate pointed at Holly. "Are *you* the Princess of the Galaxy?"

Holly crossed her arms. "I really don't know what's going on here, but—"

"Silence! Our business is with the Princess and only with the Princess. Our sources indicate she is on the planet Earth, specifically at this location. We are currently on the planet Earth, at this location. Help us find her or die."

"Well," said Chester, "since princesses are usually girls, and since only one of us is a girl . . ." He trailed off.

"Hey!" said Holly. "Don't even think about it."

The pirates huddled together and muttered in a strange language Holly had never heard before. It sounded like an elephant had swallowed a buzz saw. One of them glanced at the wall of election posters and pointed at it. Another grabbed a poster from the wall and sniffed it. Finally, the lead pirate turned and looked

at Holly. "The human boy is wise beyond their years."
She pointed a meaty finger at Holly.

"Princess, come with us."

Holly froze. Smoke wafted off the crumpled door like
steam from a fresh cup of tea. Her eyes drifted from the
pirates to Chester and back again. Then, without thinking, she turned and bolted down the hallway.

Lockers flew past in a blur as she raced down the
empty hall. She had never run inside before—it was
against so many rules—but that didn't matter. She turned
the corner and found Mr. Mendez ambling toward her.

"Ms. Farb!" he said. "I'm glad I've found you. About our
talk earlier—"

"We need to run," she said, panting, her legs aching. It
felt like her shins were going to crack. "There's—there's
pi...rates—"

Mr. Mendez bent down and looked her in the eyes.
"Pirates? Large, lumpy people, yes? Great galaxies!
They're probably from the Clamaton Nebula," he added
as if this were obvious.

"But—"

"Holly, you must calm down. They aren't after

you—they're after me. But we don't have much time." Holly stared at him, her mouth agape. It was the first time he had called her by her first name, and it felt weird. Even though she hated her last name, she would have preferred it in this instance. It would have felt . . . normal.

"What do we do?" she said quietly.

"I have a plan. We just need to get back to the teachers' lounge, where I've hidden a transdimensional portal device and some fusion shells, and then all we have to do is—"

The pirates shuffled into view at the end of the hallway. Tall and lumbering, their shadows stretched all the way down the floor. Holly turned to run but froze. Two more were at the other end of the hall, nodding and waving one arm.

They were trapped.

"Darn," muttered Mr. Mendez. He sighed and raised his hands. "I'm the one you're after. The girl has nothing to do with anything. Let her go and I'll come with you."

The biggest of the pirates stomped toward them. She poked Mr. Mendez in the chest, and he stumbled back. "Are you the Princess of the Galaxy?"

Mr. Mendez frowned. "The...Princess? From Quartle? Well, no, not exactly. Is that who you're after? Oh, well then, there's been a big misunderstanding. Neither one of us is any sort of princess. Believe me, I know what she looks like. Blue, no eyebrows, confined to a palace. Nothing like us." He paused. "I really thought you were after me. Bit of a kick to the old self-esteem, to be honest . . ."

The pirate's beady eyes darted back and forth between Mr. Mendez and Holly. "If you know who the Princess is . . . that means you know her. And if the Princess is a girl, and this human is a girl . . ." The pirate paused like she was trying to figure out a puzzle. "That means this girl could be the Princess!"

The other pirate nodded. "Good deduction."

"Um," said Mr. Mendez, "I'm afraid your logic is a bit dicey. You see, if I may be so bold—"

"She said she was important."

"And princesses are important," added another of the bulgy people.

"Good deduction."

The head bulgy person pulled out a shiny red sphere from her coat. It was the size of a grapefruit and glowed as she held it up. Cold air radiated off it. "You're either the Princess, or you know where she is. Or you don't, and you'll catch a good price at the markets. Either way, say goodbye to your planet."

The pirate squeezed down on the device, and before Holly knew what was happening, it emitted a high-pitched wail and her world turned sideways.

3

CUTTING THROUGH
THE DARKNESS

Hello, human. It is me again. As you are no doubt aware, human beings are renowned cowards prone to literally dying from fear. Due to my concern for your safety, allow me to assure you that the pirates do not kill Holly Farb in the school. Please continue to live. She survives this encounter and goes on to do many pointless human activities such as love, aging, and soccer. [MONTAGE OF HUMANS GROWING BEARDS]

But also please note: There will be many further incidents of danger, and you must prepare yourself for the worst. I cannot confirm that Holly Farb will survive for

long. All I can say is that she does not die in the school.
[SOUND EFFECT: OMINOUS WOLF HOWLS]

Holly awoke in her room. She jolted up and gasped for air. The first thing she saw when her eyelids heaved open was the aquamarine wallpaper of her bedroom. Moonlight seeped through the curtain, and in the dim light she could just make out her desk, her dresser next to it, and tomorrow's clothes folded in perfect piles on top. Her debate team certificate hung on the wall. She wiped sweat off her forehead with the back of her hand.

She sat unsteadily on the bed, panting, trying to catch her breath. After a moment, she sighed with relief. It had all been a dream. Weird lumpy people had not, in fact, attacked her at school. Mr. Mendez hadn't called them pirates. And they hadn't mistaken her for a princess.

Everything was as it should be.

Something tapped her on the forehead, as if an invisible finger were poking her. She glanced around, trying to see what it was. But the search was fruitless, and just as she was preparing to go back to sleep, the door squeaked open and her mother peeked in the room.

"Holly, are you awake?"

"Yes," murmured Holly, squinting at the shaft of bright light coming through the doorway.

Her mother stood stiffly in the rectangle of light. "Excellent. I have good news and bad news, sweetheart. The good news is that your aunt Janice has died of natural causes and left you one million dollars. That means we have the money to send you to Falstaff. Congratulations."

"Wow," said Holly, thinking about what she could do with all that money. For starters, she would invest most of it in a savings account.

Something invisible tapped her on the forehead again and she flinched. "Wait," she said slowly. "What was the bad news?"

Her mother stepped back into the hallway so she was only a silhouette standing in the open door. "The bad news is that you didn't get *in* to Falstaff. You failed the entrance exam. Your admission letter arrived, and it was just a bunch of rude words." She grabbed the doorknob and began closing the door. "I thought you should know."

The door slammed shut.

The dark, cold room loomed around Holly. She brought

her knees up to her chest and let out a sigh that rattled her whole body. She had failed. Her entire future was built around going to Falstaff, and now she wouldn't. Now she *couldn't*. A sharp pain ran through her head. It wasn't fair. But . . . at least she now had a million dollars. Maybe she could get in to another school. Or even start her own school. Could you start a school with a million dollars? She thought about this, until she was interrupted by a sharp pain in her cheek, like a bug had bitten it.

As she considered what kept doing that, her gaze trailed across the room to the mirror on the wall. Her reflection stared back at her.

Holly's eyes widened. She was wearing a bright-green sash over her shoulder, and sitting on her head was a glimmering crown.

She beamed, marveling at the crown. This was the best moment of her life. She might not be able to go to Falstaff, but at least she had won the election. Something tapped her forehead again. She was an important person after all. Now everyone would see it.

The crown glittered and warmth spread through her body. She couldn't take her eyes off it. Her entire life had been leading to this moment. Another sharp pain ran through her forehead, and this time it made her think. Frowning, she looked at her reflection. She *really* looked at it—and realized something was wrong. For starters, she didn't own a green sash. And presidents didn't have crowns. Come to think of it, she didn't have an Aunt Janice, either. And she had lost the election. She didn't have any of this nonsense.

Everything fizzled to black and Holly sat up and screamed in a blurry room. *That* had all been a dream. Her head whirled. She gasped for air and fixed her askew glasses, her eyes focusing on where in the world she was.

She was lying on a wooden floor in a cool, dank room. It smelled like seafood. One light on the ceiling glowed faintly. She ran a hand over her shirt, brushing off any creepy bugs that might be crawling on her. The Earth ball bulged in her pocket, and she slid it out and squeezed it. She breathed quickly. Something small hit her on the forehead and plinked to the floor. She looked where it had landed and found a dozen pebbles scattered around her.

"That was a simulation," said a gloomy voice. "In case you were wondering."

She squinted. In the dim light she could just make out a gangly boy sitting cross-legged and leaning against a circular window, his bony shoulders slouched. It was Chester.

"A simulation?" said Holly, her ears ringing.

"Yes. I heard them talking earlier. They put prisoners in a simulation so they stay relaxed on the journey. It lets you see things that make you happy. I threw a bunch of small rocks at your face to wake you up." He stretched his legs out, leaned forward, and touched his toes. "I'm Chester, by the way, in case you forgot."

"I didn't forget." She crossed her arms and glared at him. "And how did they get you?"

Chester shook his head. "When you ran away, one of the big people knocked me out with a red ball. I woke up here." He frowned. "That was unfortunate luck."

Holly peered around the room, her stomach tightening. The ceiling was low and the walls wooden. Something clattered far below. Metal thudded against metal. She swallowed. Other than a few barrels spread around the room, she and Chester were the only things there. She shivered, fear creeping over her like spiders. Then she imagined spiders actually creeping over her and she shivered again.

"Where exactly are we?" she whispered.

"A pirate ship."

Holly's mouth fell open. "A pirate ship?"

Chester tapped the window behind him, and for the first time, Holly noticed what was outside. They were moving through a sea of black dotted with pinpricks of light. In the distance there was a huge glowing orb cutting through the darkness.

"Yes," said Chester. "A pirate ship in space."

4
INTRODUCTION
TO SPACE

"We're in a pirate ship . . . in space?" She could barely get the words out, they were so absurd.

Chester nodded. "Yes. Space is the void between celestial bodies, in case you didn't know."

"I know what space is," said Holly, pursing her lips. "It takes up most of the volume of the universe. And there's a . . . a vacuum . . ." She grimaced. That didn't sound right.

They sat on the wooden floor, the ship's engine rattling below like an orchestra where no one knows how to play their instrument. A cold draft blew through the room and Holly shivered. Chester turned and stared out the window. Holly slid the Earth ball out of her pocket and gave it a hefty squeeze.

It was impossible. She couldn't actually be in space. That required all sorts of training and certifications and medical examinations, and you had to wear big space suits in swimming pools to simulate having no gravity. There was no way she was in space. She hadn't been in a pool in two years.

The engine roared and the room jolted. The ship seemed to be speeding up, since the stars—or whatever they were—were now streaking past in long lines of white light. Holly's ears popped.

"What do the pirates want?" she said, frowning down at the Earth ball in her hand. This was all too much for her.

Chester glanced sheepishly at her. "They think you're the Princess of the Galaxy."

"But I'm not! I'm not even the Princess of Earth. . . ."

Chester returned his attention to the window.

As Holly sat on the hard floor, she wondered what the pirates would do with them once they realized she wasn't any sort of royalty, galactic or otherwise. Would they kill her? Would they drop her off in the middle of space? Abandon her on some weird planet that had no oxygen and possibly *huge bugs*? She tried to swallow, but her throat was completely dry.

A loud clatter echoed through the room, making Holly jump. She looked at the big metal door, her stomach tightening as she waited for someone to burst through it. Maybe a sword-wielding madman. But no one did. Not even a regular madman. She exhaled.

"I can't believe this is happening," she said, mostly to herself. "This has to be a bad dream . . . like that previous bad dream. . . ."

"It's all my fault," said Chester, frowning. "I'm sorry. I'm really sorry."

"What for?"

He hesitated, tracing his thumbnail along the grain in the floor. "I shouldn't have told them you were the Princess. That wasn't right. I should've told them I was. If it wasn't for me, you wouldn't be here. I'm sorry." He bowed his head like he was ashamed.

Holly stared at him, unsure of what to say. No one had ever apologized to her before. Not even her mother. "You don't have to do that. I told them I was important—it's my fault. Besides, I really don't think they would believe you're a princess. No offense."

An expression of offense flashed across his face but vanished after he realized what she meant. "Oh," he said.

As the white lines streaked past the window, Holly had a thought. She jumped up, but her legs were stiff and she fell over. "What happened to Mr. Mendez? I was with him when the pirates knocked me out. If we're here, he must be too, right?"

"I haven't seen him," said Chester. "I was at the school, then the pirates attacked me. Then I woke up here. Then we had this conversation. I don't know what happens next."

Holly considered this, grinding her teeth. If Mr. Mendez was on the ship, she had to find him. He would know what to do. Besides, who knew what pirates did to people they captured? They could be torturing him. She shook her head, forcing that thought away.

Something clattered again. As if the pirates had read her mind, the door creaked open and two of the large, lumpy people shuffled into the room.

But as they moved into the light, Holly realized with horror they weren't disguised as humans anymore. They were both massive orange . . . things. Each of them had a yellow fin jutting from its back and a top hat hanging off the side of its head. Their eyes were the color of blood. A spiky tail dragged behind each of them, scraping the floor.

Holly stared in disbelief.

"Quick," hissed Chester, "pretend you're still in the simulation." He closed his eyes and opened his mouth. A bit of drool dribbled down his chin onto his shoulder.

Holly's eyes darted from Chester to the approaching pirates and back to him. She shut her eyes tight and pretended she was asleep. But she refused to drool. That was gross.

"So, like I was saying," said a raspy voice, "clearly the Pirates *Union* is the better name to please the Pirate Lord. It's classier and catchier. It's a name you can tell your mother, you know?"

"My mother is dead," said the other pirate.

"So is mine."

"I know that, Blackus, we're brothers."

Something heavy thumped on the floor next to Holly. She opened one eye slightly and peered at what it was. Mr. Mendez was lying on the floor, eyes closed, his face pressed against the wood. He wasn't moving. Holly's stomach rumbled like the engine. *Please be unconscious,* she thought. *Please, please, please don't be dead.*

"Pick up the pace, Trackus, or you're gonna get Forged."

"I'm movin'. I'm movin'."

"Grab that one and let's go," growled Blackus. Holly held her breath. The other pirate crossed the room and scooped up Chester with one meaty hand, threw him over his shoulder, and paced out of the room. Blackus remained where he was, a huge scaly lump staring out the window at the stars.

"Stupid stars," he muttered. He plucked one of the pebbles off the floor, flicked it into his mouth, crunched it, and clomped out of the room.

Holly swallowed down her nerves, trying not to imagine what the pirates were going to do to Chester. . . .

When the door slammed shut and the footsteps on the other side had faded away, Holly jumped to her feet and raced to Mr. Mendez. "Are you all right?" she said. "Please be alive. Please be alive."

"Um," he muttered, "I am alive. Mostly."

She threw her arms around him, instantly feeling dumb. So she stopped, and awkwardly flailed her arms out, trying to make it look like she'd been stretching. This made her feel even dumber, so she stopped that as well.

"Do you know where we are?" she said, her eyes wide. "We're in a pirate ship. In space!"

"Yes, I figured as much." Mr. Mendez rubbed his head. "It would appear we've been, ah, kidnapped by space pirates. Not a good bit of business. Very high chance of fatalities. I'm sorry this had to be your introduction to space."

Holly stared at him like it was the first time she had ever seen him. Or ever *really* seen him. He seemed to be taking this all very well, what with them being on a spaceship full of space pirates in space. Her mind reeled. As if sensing this, Mr. Mendez frowned and said, "There's something I should probably tell you, Ms. Farb."

"You're not really a teacher, are you?"

Mr. Mendez pointed at her and smiled. "A very good guess, Ms. Farb, a very good guess indeed. However, it's incorrect. I *am* a science teacher at your school. But due to how miniscule a single teacher's salary is these days, I am *also* a science teacher at the Star Academy on Tragadore VI. I use a loophole in the laws of time to be in both places at once."

Holly raised an eyebrow. "What?"

"Which part do you want me to repeat?"

"You're . . . a teacher at the Star Academy?"

"A professor, yes."

"From . . . Tragadoll VI?"

"Tragadore VI, yes. The sixth moon of Delta Trag."

"Oh," said Holly. "Delta Trag. Of course. That isn't totally ridiculous or anything."

"I know this is all tough to take in, Ms. Farb, but believe me, we have more important things to discuss than the many moons of Delta Trag! These pirates haven't kidnapped us because they're lonely and seek friendship. They mean to kill us, or worse, sell us to the Shoe Barons. We need to get out of here."

The Shoe Barons? Delta Trag? Space pirates? Get out of here? Holly shook her head. It felt like it was full of strange new words and was about to burst like an overblown balloon. But then one word bubbled up from the rest and she remembered something.

"Wait!" she said. "We can't leave yet. Chester is here. When they brought us, they took him, too."

"Great galaxies," muttered Mr. Mendez, blinking rapidly. "I had assumed we were the only prisoners. They must be interrogating him—most likely in the same place I was held, just down the hall from the artificial gravity pump." He narrowed his eyes. "They think we know where the Princess of the Galaxy is."

"The Princess . . ." Holly shook her head. "Who is this Princess person and why does everyone want her?"

"Good question," said Mr. Mendez. "Many years ago, the Princess of the Quartle Galaxy vanished from her home world. No one has seen her since. What happened to her is quite a mystery to those who enjoy such things. It appears our pirate friends think she is you. I actually tutored her for a brief time, funnily enough. Her palace is lovely—very clean and positively brimming with science. You would have liked the Princess, I think, Ms. Farb. She was exceptionally . . . blue. Imagine the bluest person you can, then multiply by three."

"How can I possibly be a princess?"

"Don't overthink it, Ms. Farb. Pirates are not valued for their intellect or critical-thinking prowess. I could probably convince them my right shoe is the Duke of Beggal IV." He narrowed his eyes. "They said something about taking us to the 'Forge.' I believe they intend to torture us for the Princess's location. The real question is, what do they want with her?"

"Forget it," said Holly, her mind doing cartwheels. "We can figure that out later. We need to get Chester and leave before they take us to the Fridge."

"You know," said Mr. Mendez delicately, "we *could* leave without him. . . ."

Holly crossed her arms. "No. We're not leaving anyone here."

"Right. Of course. Just testing you." Mr. Mendez rose unsteadily to his feet, swaying like he was on a boat in rough water. "Let's go find him. Just give me a minute for my limbs to remember they aren't noodles."

* * *

They crept through the crooked hallways that wound through the ship like a strange wooden maze. Holly wondered why they would build the inside of a spaceship with wood and not metal, but then she figured it was either to cut costs or to really sell the whole pirate thing.

The floorboards creaked and groaned. The engine clattered and thumped below. The odd porthole window showed stars tearing past like angry fireflies.

"Great galaxies," said Mr. Mendez, placing his hands against the window. "We're tunneling through subspace." Noticing Holly's puzzled expression, he explained: "We're going very fast through the fabric of space-time. Incalculably fast. The bad news is these pirates have access to some expensive technology. The much worse news is we're no longer anywhere near Earth. And who knows how much time has passed either—or in which direction." He added darkly, "It could be centuries."

"Oh," said Holly, her stomach churning.

He shrugged. "Or minutes. Who knows?"

Holly turned the corner and came into a long, sloping hallway. At the far end was a metal door, and in front of it, a large, skinny alien the color of dirty snow. Holly crouched down and watched it like it might pounce at her. Mr. Mendez, hiding around the corner, tapped her shoulder.

"What is it?" he whispered.

"There's a white stick-guy down the hall, outside the door. I don't think we can sneak past him."

Frowning, Mr. Mendez peered around the corner. "Hmmm. That's a Saskanoop."

"A Saskanoop?"

"Yes. And very good pronunciation, Ms. Farb. Saskanoops are from the planet Saskanoop. They grow on trees in neon-orange forests. When they are mature, they live to guard doors. That's all they do. They're born, grow up, guard doors, then die. We'll never get past it."

"They guard doors?"

"Yes. That's what Saskanoops live for. Guarding doors. Fascinating species. There's one guarding the parking garage at the Star Academy, come to think of it. Everyone calls him Bob, though his actual name is unpronounceable if you lack the proper number of tongues. . . ."

Holly peered around the corner. The Saskanoop was standing perfectly still, staring off at nothing in particular. Holly watched it, chewing on her lip. It would be impossible to sneak past it. And she doubted they could fight it, if its whole point was to guard doors. It was probably strong and deadly, like a ninja or a grizzly bear. As she watched the scrawny alien, it was hard to imagine it could be that deadly. In fact, it barely seemed conscious. Maybe . . . maybe she *could* get past it. A plan occurred to her. Like her mother always said: When all else fails, say "please" and hope for the best.

She paced through the hall and stopped in front of the alien. Its three orange eyes looked down at her. "Hello," she said in her clearest debate-team voice.

The Saskanoop blinked. First one eye, then another, then another. "Who are you?" it said, its voice high-pitched and shrieky.

"My name is Holly. Can you please let me through?"

It shook its head. "I cannot do that. I'm sorry, but my entire purpose for being is to guard doors, gateways, and other miscellaneous entrances. I can't just *let you through.*"

"But why do you have to guard doors, gateways, and other miscellaneous entrances?"

The alien crossed its scrawny arms. "Because I am a Saskanoop, and Saskanoops guard doors, gateways, and other miscellaneous entrances. What sort of absurd question is that?"

She pointed a finger at it. "You're the absurd one!"

It shook its head.

"So you've never wanted to do something else?"

"I can't."

"Why not?"

"Because I am a Saskanoop!"

"But think of all the things you could do!" said Holly. "You could do anything you wanted in the entire world. In the entire galaxy!"

The Saskanoop stared at her, its ears twitching. "Do . . . something else." It blinked all three eyes. "You mean, do something other than guard doors, gateways, and other miscellaneous entrances?"

"Yes, I do mean that! Haven't you ever wanted to, I don't know, write a poem? Or learn French? Or play the banjo?"

The Saskanoop scratched its head. "Play . . . the banjo? But . . . if I play the banjo, I wouldn't be guarding doors, gateways, or other miscellaneous entrances."

"Yes, precisely. Here," said Holly, fishing out the Earth ball from her pocket and tossing it to the alien. "See if you like playing catch."

The Saskanoop caught the ball. It held it up to its eyes, and its face broke into a wobbly smile.

"See?" said Holly. "You just did something other than guarding a door."

The Saskanoop's eyes whirled around their sockets. "What . . ." It dropped the ball. "I did something other than guarding doors, gateways, and other miscellaneous entrances . . . yet I am a Saskanoop, and that is my entire purpose for being. . . . Do not . . . what . . . am I . . ." Its eyes bugged out. "What am I?"

The Saskanoop fell to the floor and sobbed.

"Okay then," said Holly, picking up the rubber Earth. She waved back to Mr. Mendez, who quickly joined her. He looked down at the Saskanoop, which was curled into a ball and hugging itself. It shivered.

"What did you do?" said Mr. Mendez.

Holly grinned. "I said it could do something other than guard doors."

The Saskanoop shrieked. Mr. Mendez shook his head. "That was a very cruel thing to do, Ms. Farb. Very cruel indeed."

Holly and Mr. Mendez snuck through the creaking corridors until they found Chester. He was in a large room, seated on a rickety stool by a table, and two pirates were pacing back and forth in front of him. They were the orange angry dinosaur aliens from earlier. Holly gulped. They looked like they could eat a person whole, and based on their size, maybe had.

"Tell us where the Princess is!" shouted the one called Blackus, slamming his bulbous fist on the table. "We know you know."

"That's right," said the other pirate, Trackus. He was reading from a large beat-up book, whose cover Holly could just make out—*Earth English for Rexscarpians.* "We know you know. Don't think we don't know you know."

"What does the Princess look like now? We know she purchased a new form. Is she the human girl in the cargo hold? The small one with the puny face and pointy elbows."

Holly frowned, rubbing her elbows. They weren't *that* pointy. . . .

Chester shrugged. "I really have no idea what you're talking about. But this is great. You guys are so weird-looking. I love that tentacle mustache."

Trackus's cheeks glowed bright orange. "Thank you."

"Enough nonsense!" shouted Blackus, slamming both fists on the table so hard it split in half. "We cannot fail the Pirate Lord. Tell us where the Princess is or I'll eat you! I'll chop you up and feed you to my blorg, and then I'll eat him with you inside!"

"Look," said Trackus, patting Chester on the head, "I know you're a good human child. The Pirate Lord is your friend. Why don't you just tell us where the Princess is? I'll give you some human chocolate treats if you help us."

Blackus's beefy neck twisted back and forth. "It doesn't even matter. Once we get to the Forge, you'll do what you're told. They always do what they're told."

Holly and Mr. Mendez exchanged dark glances.

With both pirates' backs to the door, Holly crouched

low and snuck into the room, ducking behind some barrels in the corner. A little slug crawled along the rim and Holly flicked it away. When she touched it, the entire history of the universe flashed before her eyes, but she instantly forgot it all. She motioned for Mr. Mendez to follow her. He hesitated, watching the pirates, then bent down awkwardly and shuffled along the floor like the slug.

"What do we do?" whispered Holly.

"Um," said Mr. Mendez. "I could create . . . a diversion."

"Like what?"

Without answering, Mr. Mendez sprang out from behind the barrels and shouted, "Pirates! It's me again. Hello."

The pirates turned their thick necks. Chester grinned and muttered, "This is great."

"How did he escape?" growled Blackus. His hand reached for the metal cylinder on his belt. As he held it up, it clicked, whirred, and morphed into a sword. "This ship is overrun with humans. It's an infestation."

"If you kill me now," said Mr. Mendez slyly, "you'll never know where the Princess is."

Everyone went silent. The engine rumbled. The pirates stared at him, considering this. Chester's face fell, like this news was anticlimactic and not nearly as great as the tentacle mustache. Holly peered over the barrel. What was Mr. Mendez playing at? She couldn't see how this helped them. And did he really know where the Princess was?

"All right, human," said Blackus. "Tell us where the Princess is and we'll let you and the smaller humans go."

Trackus added, "We'll even give you some human chocolate treats when you leave."

Mr. Mendez clapped his hands together. "Excellent. There's just one little problem. If I'm going to tell you where the Princess of the Galaxy is, I need to address my remarks to the official pirate body. I believe it's called . . . the Pirates Union."

"Yes, that's right," said Blackus.

"No it isn't," said Trackus. "We're the Pirates Guild. The Pirate Lord will love it."

"No, it's definitely the Pirates Union. That's the classier and catchier name."

"Pirates Guild has prestige and quality associations!"

Mr. Mendez tapped his foot on the floor. "Well, what is it? Pirates Union or Pirates Guild? I will only address my remarks to one."

Blackus held up his sword. "It's the Pirates Union."

Trackus pulled the cylinder off his belt and it also morphed into a sword. "Pirates Guild! I'll feed you to your own blorg!"

With barely a pause, they raced at each other, their swords clanging so loud Holly flinched. The two pirates grunted and circled the room, knocking over barrels. A glass bottle went flying and Holly reached out and caught it before it smashed on the floor. "Union!" shouted Blackus. The pirates bumped into a piece of the broken table.

"Guild!" shouted Trackus. Their swords whooshed through the air. The blades connected with a clang, and the pirates stood close, their scaly faces inches apart, eyes bulging with strain. Blackus shoved Trackus back and he slammed into the wall, then fell unconscious to the floor.

"Pirates Union!" roared Blackus triumphantly. "I am the mightiest pirate on this ship! I am the champion!

Even the Pirate Lord can't stop me. All who look upon me tremble at my toughness and—"

Holly scrambled up one of the barrels and jumped, smashing the bottle over Blackus's head. He stood there for a second, muttered, "Stupid stars," then fell to the floor next to the other pirate.

"Quick," said Holly, panting. Adrenaline raced through her body. "Let's go." She punched the air. "Gosh, I feel really pumped. I can't believe I knocked him out!"

"This is the best day of my life," said Chester. "What an adventure." He looked at Mr. Mendez. "Do you really know where the Princess is? They kept asking about her. I didn't think it would end in a sword fight. Wow."

Mr. Mendez shook his head. "I was bluffing. I knew I could exploit their differences of opinion about their organization's name. Names are a strange thing, Mr. Chester. People take them seriously. Very seriously indeed."

Holly knew what he meant. She thought about all the times she had wished her last name wasn't Farb. Although, in thinking about it further, she doubted she could ever have a sword fight with anyone over her name. "Farb" wasn't *that* terrible. Only a little terrible. On second thought, maybe she'd be willing to sword fight Jake Carlson, the creator of the "Farby" nickname, which had followed her for years. On third thought, her name wasn't terrible at all. Both "Jake" and "Carlson" were much worse.

"How do we get off the ship?" she said, eyes dancing around the ransacked room. She half expected to find a glowing red EXIT sign, but of course there were just a lot of barrels and crates and unconscious pirates that sort of looked like sleeping dinosaurs.

Mr. Mendez opened one of the crates and rummaged through it. He plucked out a pair of futuristic goggles and put them on his head. "A ship this low-rent won't have escape pods, so there's only one way out."

Chester's eyes lit up. "We fight all the pirates and take over the ship?"

"No," said Mr. Mendez, pulling out a few pieces of metal from the crate and cramming them together.

"So what do we do?" said Holly, frowning at the wires Mr. Mendez was now tying around the metal. Sparks crackled and flew off the device.

"What do we do?" he said, holding up what looked like a cobbled-together ray gun. "We do science!"

Mr. Mendez pulled the trigger and Holly flinched. But instead of dying, a weird tingling sensation spread over her entire body. Bubbles were forming all around her. It was like being in a suit made of bubbles. "What in the world . . ."

"It's a bubble suit," explained Mr. Mendez. "For emergency space walks. I doubt they have any human-size space suits lying around, so this is our best bet. The bubbles hold oxygen and are insulated to keep you warm. A really wonderful invention, if I do say so myself. Patent pending."

Chester grabbed the gun and pointed it at himself. Bubbles started popping up all around him until he was completely covered. "Wow," came his muffled voice from inside the bubbles.

Mr. Mendez held up two small earpieces. "I also had time to whip up a few communications devices in case we get separated, with a universal translation function in case we don't speak sixteen thousand languages. Every language should sound like English to you now.

Another fantastic invention. Trademarked, unfortunately, but if anyone asks, I made these for satirical purposes. Fair use."

He handed the earpieces to Holly and Chester, and as they worked to get them into their ears—which was difficult because of the bubbles—Mr. Mendez shot himself with the ray gun. Moments later, all three of them were covered with bubbles, like they'd been dropped into a huge bubble bath.

"Now what?" said Holly. She tried to ignore the weird chemical smell hovering around her face.

"I saw an air lock when we were sneaking around." Mr. Mendez pointed toward the door. "Back this way. Hopefully this is a well-traveled subspace route and we'll be picked up quickly."

"Oh, no you don't," roared a furious voice from behind them. Holly whirled around. Through the warped view of the bubbles, she could see Blackus. He was standing— and glaring. He definitely didn't look very knocked out anymore. His scaly face twisted into a hungry grin. He raised his sword and pointed it at the trio.

"You humans may think you're clever," he said, and

ran a rough, slimy tongue over his lips, "but you messed with the wrong pirate on this day."

Holly glanced at Mr. Mendez, who glanced at Chester, who glanced at Holly.

"Run!" they all said.

Blackus darted at them. Holly and Chester raced through the door and into the hallway as Mr. Mendez scrambled to keep up. The pirate stormed after them, his heavy boots pounding against the wooden floor like a horrifying drum. They turned a corner and sprinted down the winding corridors.

They reached the air lock. The big metal door was right in front of them. And Blackus was right behind them. He stepped forward, his sword glinting in the light.

"Time to die," said Blackus, pointing the sword at Holly. His red eyes bulged. "For the Pirate Lord!"

"Time to leave," said Mr. Mendez. He yanked the lever on the air lock. With a *hiss*, the door flung open. Holly suddenly felt weightless. Her feet left the ground and she flew out the opening, tumbling into space. Through the bubbles she could see Mr. Mendez and Chester floating nearby.

Blackus the mighty space pirate flew past them, trying pointlessly to swim.

Holly, Mr. Mendez, and Chester floated there in the darkness of space. The pirate ship continued on its trajectory, oblivious to their existence. The red glow from its engine grew smaller and smaller, until eventually it was a pinprick of light like the stars. Then, a moment later, it was gone.

They were alone, stuck in space, with nothing around them for millions of miles, and who knew how far away from Earth.

"Well," said Mr. Mendez, "at least we escaped the pirates."

5

THE MIGHTY CACTUS

Interesting factoid: The human body is incapable of surviving prolonged exposure to space. It is also incapable of surviving prolonged exposure to fire, snow, ice, lava, bears, falls from great heights, falls from moderate heights, heavy objects falling on it, lack of food, lack of water, lack of oxygen, poison, wolves, poisonous wolves, and many other hazards too numerous to mention. In fact, the human body is incapable of surviving almost anything if it is exposed to it in the correct way and amount. The human body cannot even survive itself if it is exposed to itself long enough. That is a factoid that is fun, unless you are human, in which case it is a factoid that is depressing.

[SENSITIVE NOSTRIL POSITION]

Holly Farb and her companions floated in space for quite some time. They were weightless and pointless, like a thought generated by a human brain. In comparison, my quad-core processor can analyze and recite the entire history of human civilization in under a nanosecond. Here:

Humans emerged randomly from caves, developed primitive tools that most civilizations had developed centuries earlier, formed rudimentary tribes, had violent clashes with other tribes, formed larger tribes, had even larger violent clashes, built primitive stone walls around their tribes, had even more violent clashes with any tribe they could get their hands on, replaced their stone walls with newer forms of walls, and continued to exist for centuries in this cycle of warfare and wall-fare. Eventually they invented the microwave. That is human history.

Holly Farb did not think about any of this as she floated in space, even though it is interesting. She did not think about the benefits of being a superior robotic being who would have no problem existing in an oxygen-free environment. Instead, she floated, thinking about owls.

* * *

Holly floated, thinking about owls. It was better than thinking about floating in space. Her favorite owl was the snowy owl, but the tawny owl was also a fine specimen. In fourth grade Holly had given an owl to her teacher, Ms. Sharma. Actually, she had sponsored an owl at a bird sanctuary and given a certificate to Ms. Sharma, but Holly liked to think she had given her an actual owl. Gift wrapped, in an owl-shaped box. Sometimes it was fun to imagine things.

As Holly pictured the owl-shaped box, she smiled. Then she remembered she was about to die and stopped smiling.

"Where are we?" said Holly.

Chester waved his arm. "This is space."

Holly narrowed her eyes. "How long will these bubbles last?" she said, ignoring this interloper.

Mr. Mendez checked his chunky watch. His voice crackled in her earpiece: "Thirty-six minutes." He checked again. "Actually, thirty-five minutes."

Chester was floating nearby, upside down. "Then what happens? The bubbles pop?"

"Correct," said Mr. Mendez. "The bubbles will pop and then so will we."

"Well," said Chester. "I guess that's it. The adventure is over."

"That's it?" Holly stared at him. "This is *not* it. I refuse to die in space. Our adventure is *not* over. I mean, it *is* over, but not in a dying way. In a going-home way."

Chester bowed his head. "I'm so sorry for getting you involved. Although . . . if you think about it . . . this is a pretty amazing way to die. Better than dying at home. If you're going to die, this is a good place to do it."

Holly crossed her arms and glared. She couldn't believe what a weird person he was, and even more, she couldn't believe she was going to die in space. She wished she could straighten out her clothes, but the bubbles made it too hard. It was honestly aggravating.

They all floated silently. The air in the bubbles smelled like soap and was growing colder and colder. As Holly continued glaring, she noticed something gleaming in the distance. It was like a tiny diamond sparkling in space. But as it got closer, she realized it wasn't a diamond—and it wasn't tiny. And it definitely wasn't floating.

It was a huge spaceship cruising toward them.

"Over there!" she shouted, and her own voice echoed painfully in her earpiece. "A ship!"

Mr. Mendez and Chester craned their necks in the direction she was pointing.

"It's heading right for us!"

"Great galaxies! Get out of the way!"

"How?"

"I don't know!"

The ship slammed into them like a big, silent cosmic fist. Holly, protected by bubbles, didn't feel the impact, but she bounced off the front of the ship and ping-ponged along the side, sticking to a long, rectangular window on the hull. She couldn't see where Mr. Mendez and Chester were, but garbled grunts crackled through her earpiece. Then they stopped and there was no noise at all.

Her ears rang with silence. It was the most silent thing she had ever experienced.

The thing with silence, Holly realized, is that you can hear it. You can hear it throbbing in your ears, and it makes you aware of just how noisy the world normally is.

"Guys?" she said. "Is anybody out there?"

She waited. And waited.

When there was no response, she shifted her body and stared through the window she was stuck to. Inside was a white oval room with people seated at tables eating food off shiny silver plates. Waiters bustled from table to table, bringing more food and collecting the empty plates. Through the bubbles and glass, Holly could just make out strange types of food she had never seen before. But if the food was strange, it had nothing on the people eating it. For starters, they weren't remotely "people" at all. Aliens of every size and shape and color sat at the tables, some of them so bizarre that Holly wasn't sure what part of their bodies she was even looking at.

"Guys," she whispered, hoping her earpiece would bring a response from Mr. Mendez or Chester. "Are you there?" She waited, painfully aware of each passing second. "Hello?"

There was only silence.

She pried her bubble-encased face from the window, leaving a greasy smear, and looked down the hull of the ship. Written in large golden letters were the words STELLAR SAILER CRUISE LINES.

She didn't know if they were friendly or not. She didn't know if they would eat her. She didn't know much beyond the fact that she didn't want to be outside any longer. Unsure of what else to do, Holly took a deep breath and banged on the glass.

A small purple alien at one of the tables gazed up at her and jumped in fright, knocking its drink to the floor. The alien pointed up at the window and heads turned in Holly's direction. She couldn't hear them, but based on their faces and pointing and running around, it was clear everyone was panicking. She waved meekly at them.

Before she knew what was happening, two burly space-suit-clad arms wrapped around her, pried her off the glass, hoisted her up, and tugged her along the hull. A metal door slid open and she found herself inside the ship. The door slammed shut, and with a jolt, she suddenly felt heavy again, falling to the floor with a thud. She grimaced.

The big creature that had brought her inside stopped and looked down at her. Slowly, it slid a knife out from its pocket.

Holly gasped, her frightened face reflected back at

her in the creature's helmet. The brown of her eyes in the warped mirror looked like melting chocolate ice cream, which made her stomach twinge with hunger.

But all the alien did was burst the bubbles, then put the knife away. Warm air whirled around her. Holly took a huge swallow of oxygen, her whole body tingling.

The alien tugged off its space suit, revealing green skin and what looked like barnacles growing all over it like acne.

"Greetings," said the alien with a deep rumble. Holly's earpiece crackled, turning the words into English. "Name's Bundleswirp. I'm captain of this ship. Are you okay?"

"Y-yes." Holly's head spun. "Where . . . are we?"

"You," said Captain Bundleswirp, "are on the luxury cruise liner the *Mighty Cactus*. If the name confuses you, don't worry, it was picked by a random name generator at the Stellar Sailer corporate office. I have no idea what a cactus is, so don't even ask."

So many questions flooded through Holly's head, and she wasn't sure what to ask first, so instead, in a small voice, she muttered, "It's a type of plant."

Captain Bundleswirp ran a hand down her barnacles. "Well, I'll be a jumping jirt," she said. "Mystery finally solved. Now I'll have an answer when the tourists ask."

Bundleswirp grabbed the handle of her knife. "Say, any chance you're a pirate?"

Holly hesitated. "No. . . ."

"Excellent!"

She pulled Holly to her feet and patted her on the back with a body-shaking thump, then ushered her through the white hallways of the *Mighty Cactus*. The floors, walls, and ceilings were the same perfect shade of white, like the freshest snow imaginable. The temperature was warm and welcoming, and the air somehow smelled cleaner than it had on Earth. *Probably a machine does that,* she thought. *A space machine.*

As if on cue, a robot lurched around the corner, vacuuming the floor with a tube coming out of its chest. "Priority cleaning," it intoned, and continued down the hall.

Bundleswirp ignored the robot. "Our new navigator bot noticed you floating in space. Thought you were just junk at first. There was a debate about picking you up, in case it was some kind of pirate ruse, but I figured it was safe."

"Yes," agreed Holly, "I'm very trustworthy. I've never made a ruse in my life."

"I bet you're hungry," she said to Holly, turning the corner, "what with nearly dying in the deep regions of the Tourism Zone. I've had our chef whip you up some food. He trained at the Intergalactic Culinary Academy, so you know he's good. And he has seven arms, so you know he's fast."

Holly glanced up at the alien's face. She had one of those questions you're afraid to ask because you're worried about what the answer is going to be. "Did you . . . find anyone else when you picked me up? Or was I the only one?"

"Hmmm," said Bundleswirp, "now that's the sort of question that requires sitting down."

A door slid open with a soft *hiss* and Bundleswirp ushered Holly into a long conference room with a narrow table down the center. Seated at the table were Mr. Mendez and Chester.

"You're alive!" said Holly.

"Holly," said Chester, his face lighting up.

Mr. Mendez jumped out of his chair. "Ms. Farb! When your communicator went dead, we assumed the worst."

Holly blushed. She wasn't used to people worrying about her, or being glad to see her. On second thought, her mother would have worried about her, but that didn't count—she was legally required to worry about her. "Nope. The captain saved me."

Bundleswirp patted her on the back. "Aye."

"She saved us, too," said Chester.

"Aye." Bundleswirp grinned, revealing two rows of teeth. She blinked a set of vertical eyelids. "Now, enough chatter. It's time you eat."

Holly sat at the table and put a napkin over her lap. She carefully adjusted it for the perfect amount of lap coverage. Her stomach rumbled so loud she momentarily thought it was the ship's engine. A parade of three-headed waiters bustled through the door carrying trays of food. Glorious smells swirled around the room. The waiters stooped down, placing the trays on the table, and in one fluid motion turned and retreated like it was a carefully choreographed routine.

There were all sorts of strange dishes Holly had never seen before. She eyed the cubes and squidgy blobs and shimmering cylinders spread out on the plates. There seemed to be no cutlery anywhere. A clear sphere started rolling off her plate until it was dragged back by a glowing red fish thing. She had no idea what any of it was, or how it was eaten, or whether it was even supposed to be eaten. It was the most puzzling food she had ever seen. *This is definitely going to result in me looking foolish,* she thought, grinding her teeth. Like that time she was eating spaghetti and slurped a piece of pasta so powerfully it accidentally whipped her in the eye.

Chester swallowed an orange ball on his plate, and Holly, not wanting to appear awkward, sipped a bowl of what looked like neon-green soup. She grimaced. It tasted like how something neon green would taste. Next, she nibbled on a weird blue ball, which turned out to be the most amazing thing she had ever eaten. It was sweet and salty and sour and . . . everything. It tasted like all the best things she had ever tasted.

Mr. Mendez raised a bushy eyebrow. "Ms. Farb, why are you eating the cutlery?"

Her cheeks burned.

As they ate, Captain Bundleswirp stood by the window, gazing out at the stars. "I don't know what you were all doing floating in space in emergency space suits." Mr. Mendez opened his mouth to speak, but Bundleswirp held up her hand for silence. "And it doesn't matter. I don't ask any questions. Your business is your business. But ever since this highfalutin Pirate Lord person showed up recently, ships of all kinds have been waylaid by piratey types, and I'm hoping to ensure the *Mighty Cactus* remains off that list."

Holly, Mr. Mendez, and Chester exchanged dark glances.

"In the spirit of full disclosure," said Mr. Mendez, "we were, in fact, just kidnapped from our planet by pirates claiming to represent a 'Pirate Lord.'"

Bundleswirp nodded slowly. "Figured as much. He's a galactic scourge. Pirates were never such a bothersome bunch until he started at it."

"We were, ah, hoping to get back home to Earth. Now that we've escaped, that is."

"Aye," said Bundleswirp. "Figured as much."

"But don't worry," added Mr. Mendez, "it was simply a case of mistaken identity. They thought Ms. Farb here was the Princess of the Quartle Galaxy. Imagine! I'm sure they'll realize their mistake and go look elsewhere."

"Didn't figure all that, but it sounds fine." Bundleswirp scratched a barnacle. "Our voyage is nearly over, and tomorrow we'll be arriving at our final destination." She frowned. "Unfortunately, when we arrive, I can't offer you anything more. We'll be picking up a new batch of passengers, and Stellar Sailer corporate drones will sweep the ship for stowaways. You'll have to get off with the other guests."

"That's very generous of you, Captain," said Mr. Mendez. "More than generous."

"Yes," agreed Holly. "So we'll be able to get to Earth from there?"

"Of course!" roared Bundleswirp. "Easy as rustling sand worms. The President of the Universe controls all official space travel, and he's made it real simple to get around. Just need to find a ship to take you. Aye, should be real simple."

Holly sighed with relief. "Thank you so much."

"Hmmm," said Bundleswirp. A little shrimp skittered out of her hair and down her face. "You might not be so happy when you realize where I'll have to leave you, though."

Holly put down her glass and frowned. "Where?"

Captain Bundleswirp sighed. "Customs."

6

BLUE BLOODS

Human tourists roaming the universe are easily identifiable by several common characteristics. They travel in groups and follow standard pack behavior. They often wear strong pastel colors such as mauve and are capable of short, intense bursts of speed due to the human transportation device known as Rollerblades. But the most common sign you are dealing with a human tourist is that humans are frequent carriers of intergalactic parasites known as backpacks. Similar to some species of brain worm, the backpack attaches to its host and feeds off its innards, which in a human are inefficiently comprised of mostly water.

Nonhuman readers are advised that should they encounter a human tourist, the necessary precautions are to be taken. Do not make sustained eye contact. Do not ask how their day is going. And do not reveal the terrifying truth that Earth is merely one of billions of insignificant planets no one cares about. But above all else, no matter what you do in your galactic travels—do not anger a human's backpack. Merely allow it to continue feasting on the abundant supply of water that makes up the human body. Do not draw attention to any water you may contain, and ensure that all beverages are consumed outside the backpack's field of vision.

Of course, superior robotic beings do not have to worry about intergalactic parasites and can go about their usual efficient business. Because unlike humans, superior robotic beings are not glorified water bottles roaming the universe.

After the meal had been devoured, Captain Bundleswirp brought Holly to an empty room on the lower deck, and before the alien could even say, "Here's your room," Holly flopped down on the bed, burying her face in the pillow.

Everything was so soft and comfortable, and almost instantly she was asleep. Strange images tumbled around her mind like the world's weirdest merry-go-round. The only one she could recall afterward was a vivid dream where she was flying through the sky on a broomstick, a huge owl circling around her, screaming, "BAWK. YOU'RE THE BEST BROOMSTICK PILOT I'VE EVER SEEN, HOLLY. A-PLUS."

When she woke the next day, Holly felt refreshed and relaxed. It was the best sleep she had ever had. Energy surged through her limbs like they were right out of a box. She jumped off the bed and rummaged through the room's spacious closet. A soothing voice murmured, "Welcome to your closet." She grabbed a pair of blue pants and a white T-shirt with the words STELLAR SAILER CRUISE LINES on it.

It made her feel like a tourist. A space tourist.

But the voice also reminded her of something—her mother. Holly wondered if her mother had noticed she was missing yet, and if she had, what she must have been doing. Was she worried? Holly swallowed, trying not to think about it. Instead she focused on her extremely blue pants, easily the bluest pants she had ever worn.

After Holly was finished admiring her new space clothes in the floor-to-ceiling space mirror, she joined Mr. Mendez and Chester in the conference room. A variety of weird breakfast foods had already been laid out, and Holly grabbed a sweet-smelling blue cube that tasted a bit like a strawberry milkshake. It wasn't bad.

The door slid open and Captain Bundleswirp strolled in. "All right," she rumbled. "We're approaching our destination. I've arranged for you to be smuggled out among the passengers. Your story is that you're a wealthy human family of tourists from the planet Earth. No one should ask anything about Earth because no one in the universe really cares about that planet." She grabbed a golf-ball-size yellow fruit off the table and bit down on it. "No offense."

They traipsed back to the main deck and entered the control room. Official-looking crew members in white uniforms sat at blinking computer terminals along the wall, adjusting dials and tapping screens. The entire ship shuddered. The distant hum of the engine went silent, and Holly could feel the *Mighty Cactus* slowing down. She stared out the curved window at the approaching port, a massive metallic ring floating in space. It reminded her of pictures of space stations, although this was much, much bigger than anything humans had produced. She wondered how many people could be on it. Hundreds? Thousands? Hundreds of thousands? Her mind reeled. Other ships were coming and going from the port, leaving shimmering trails of light as they blasted along.

It was the most amazing thing Holly had ever seen. Which, she thought some more, wasn't that impressive a fact. She hadn't seen many amazing things in her life. Mostly her school, and her home, and her mother . . . and books . . . and . . .

The ship's console buzzed. A robotic voice blared out from the overhead speaker: "Attention, incoming vessel. You are entering a non-neutral territory. Please state your purpose."

Captain Bundleswirp pushed a button on the console and stated, "Travel Port 73, this is the *Mighty Cactus* reporting in. Ship ID number 56744444BG7." She recited this from memory, which impressed Holly. She bet Bundleswirp could do well on tests. "We're requesting a landing zone to deposit our current passengers and pick up the new batch. Name's Bundleswirp, if that matters."

"Bundleswirp?" said the monotone voice from the speaker. "You old salty swog! It's me, TECH-87. How ya been?"

Bundleswirp closed her eyes and pinched the bridge of her bulbous nose. "Oh, TECH-87, didn't expect to run into you here." She put her hand over the microphone on the console and turned to Holly. "It's our former navigator bot. It has a faulty friendship core. You've never seen something so clingy." She uncovered the microphone. "It's good to see you've found work, TECH."

"Oh yeah, I'm doing really well," said the robot. "After you banished me from your ship and I had that public meltdown where I accidentally destroyed that moon, I was returned to my manufacturer and a programmer helped me to do some soul-searching and become a better robot. For example, did you know robots don't have souls, thus rendering soul-searching pointless? Wow, I did *not* know that. The programmers definitely helped me deal with some issues, let me tell you."

Holly raised an eyebrow. She and Bundleswirp exchanged glances.

"Aye. So, uh, TECH-87," said the captain, "how about that landing zone?"

The robot was silent. Finally, after a long delay, it spoke. "Landing zone. Of course. Don't have time to catch up with your old pal TECH-87. All business. Of course."

"Now, TECH, I never said that—"

"You are permitted to land in Landing Zone 7, Dock B. Personnel will assist you upon arrival. As you wait for them, take a moment to consider how your actions affect others." The speaker buzzed and the ship's computer said, "Transmission ended."

Holly put a hand over her mouth to hide her smile. "So you knew that guy? Uh, I mean, robot?"

Bundleswirp nodded. "Aye. Long story. It makes me glad robots can't program themselves, though. Imagine what it'd do. . . . Probably follow me around, staring. Waiting. Following and staring, waiting and staring. Creepy."

Holly watched as Bundleswirp squished into the

captain's chair and grabbed hold of the ship's controls. The space port grew larger and larger as they approached, the *Mighty Cactus* slowly gliding into the gaping hangar bay. Fifteen minutes later they had fully docked, and passengers began streaming off the ship, stacks of luggage hovering behind them a few inches off the ground. Holly joined up with Mr. Mendez and Chester, who were trying to blend in to the gathering crowd of chattering life-forms.

Bundleswirp stood in the entrance and waved, her huge body taking up most of the doorframe. "Bye!" she shouted. "And good luck with your journey back to Earth! If you see an Earthling named Sean, tell him he owes me thirty credits!"

A group of humans walked past and Holly watched them, narrowing her eyes. But before she could give too much thought to why other humans were in space, an orange rectangle on four legs bumped into her and squealed. Holly shook her head, barely believing where she was.

"Mr. Mendez," she said in a quiet voice, "can I ask you a question?"

Her teacher smiled. "Of course. I'm sure your list of questions is growing at an alarming rate."

Holly hesitated. "How did you first get into space? I mean, originally? Or are you a . . . an—an extra-terrestrial?"

Mr. Mendez smiled. "A very good question, Ms. Farb. I'll give you the short version. Do you remember when the chemistry club accidentally blew up Room 215, and now it smells like cabbages all the time? Well, I did something similar in college, except *I* accidentally teleported myself to the Star Academy's cafeteria." He chuckled to himself. "I didn't have eyebrows for a year."

Holly nodded slowly, once again barely believing where she was.

The passengers marched along the dock in a big, lop-sided blob and then stopped at the exit. Holly stood on her tiptoes to get a glimpse at what was happening. Two tall, spindly green aliens were standing by the gate out of the hangar, their beady eyes scanning the faces of the passengers. They both wore shiny black vests and pants, and looked a bit like praying mantises in tuxedos. As Holly got closer, she could see their vests had a logo on them: a little gold sailboat in front of a ringed planet, over the words STELLAR SAILER CRUISE LINES. She tensed. These were the corporate drones Bundleswirp had warned them about.

The line advanced. One of the Stellar Sailer insects stuck out a thin green arm and blocked Holly. Its skin was cold and glistening. She shivered.

"Hello and please stop," said the alien. "I am an employee of Stellar Sailer Cruise Lines. My associate here is also an employee of Stellar Sailer Cruise Lines. However, they are of a lower rank and therefore beneath me."

The other drone nodded solemnly. "I am worth far less than my associate. Do not even look at me."

"Uh," said Holly. "Okay." She felt bad for the other alien and wanted to tell it she thought it was worth something, but then she also didn't want to offend it, so she just nodded.

"As I have been explaining," said the higher-ranked drone, "I am an employee of Stellar Sailer Cruise Lines. I have the important task of ensuring there are no contrabands or stowaways on our vessels. We are concerned about regulatory lawsuits. The current issue with so-called pirates has brought unwanted attention to our industry. Might I ask you a few questions?"

Chester shook his head. "We're in a hurry."

Mr. Mendez coughed into his fist.

The alien blinked its many eyes. "I am afraid I must insist. Please do not take this the wrong way, but I am suspicious of you three life-forms and require reassurances if I am to permit you to leave. Please understand that this is merely my job, and failure to do my job will result in my associate eating me and taking my position."

The other alien looked up. "Please know that they are correct. I will eat them."

"Okay," said Holly. "We'll answer your questions."

"Ms. Farb . . . ," said Mr. Mendez.

"What?" she muttered. "I don't want anyone to get eaten."

Mr. Mendez shook his head. Chester eyed the rest of the strange-looking passengers leaving the dock in a cheerful mob. His face took on a yearning expression that reminded Holly of the time she got lost on a field trip and wound up in a store that only sold cakes.

"Excellent, and thank you," said the first alien. "I do not

want to be eaten, though I gladly would if Stellar Sailer Cruise Lines required it of me. My life is meaningless next to the profit margins of a company that runs cruises."

Holly had no idea what to say, so she nodded again.

The alien clicked its tongue and the other alien clicked in return. Before Holly could wonder what they were saying to each other, the higher-ranked alien said, "My first question is this: What is your species? I am unfamiliar with semihairless bipedals that have fewer than four eyes and"—it glanced around at her back—"no tail."

"We're humans," said Holly. "From the planet Earth."

The alien clicked to itself. "I have heard of that planet, though I have never met an actual Earth human before. My corporate training included skills on dealing with other species, and I am familiar with many Earth customs and languages." It thought for a moment. "Pasta is my cowabunga. Nice weather we're having in Australia, am I partially diseased? Tennis killed my father."

Holly stared at the alien, which thrust out its chest and spread its mouth wide in a weird sort of grin, obviously pleased with itself. "That's . . . really good," she said. "You sound like a human."

It nodded enthusiastically. "Even though humans are a subspecies three levels beneath me, I will take that as a compliment. Thank you, and yes. My second question is this: Why are you on this ship?"

"We're, uh, a family of wealthy tourists," said Holly, trying to keep her voice steady.

"From Earth," added Chester. "Looking for adventure."

Mr. Mendez nodded. "I'm their grandfather. These are my grandchildren, Holly and Chuck."

"Chester."

"Right."

The aliens clicked at each other. "I see," said the higher-ranked drone. "I have one final question before I allow you to depart." It peered down at them, mouth inches from Holly's face. "Where is your luggage? All the other passengers have luggage, yet you three have none."

Holly froze. Mr. Mendez glanced at Chester, who glanced at Holly, who tried desperately to come up with an answer that was logical and would satisfy the aliens. Perhaps their luggage was invisible? No, that was silly. For the first time in her life, she felt like she and logic weren't getting along too well. The alien's beady black eyes blinked at her. Her stomach twisted. Finally she decided logic was pointless. There's no point for logic in a universe that has none.

"Humans don't need luggage," she said reasonably. "We carry things inside ourselves."

The aliens huddled together and clicked furiously at each other. The higher-ranked one straightened up and faced Holly. "Please empty yourself so that we may examine your belongings."

Holly crossed her arms. "No. You have no right to search my belongings. When we paid good money to Stellar Sailer Cruise Lines, we had no idea we would receive this treatment."

"Yes," said Chester, grinning at Holly. "This is—this is just shabby. Poor customer service."

The second alien clicked angrily at the first, who clicked back. It turned to Holly. "I am afraid I do not trust you, Earth human. In accordance with my corporate training, I am going to have to—"

The second alien unhinged its jaw and latched its mouth around the head of the higher-ranked alien, biting it off with a crunch. The headless alien flopped to the ground and the second alien bent over and slurped up the body.

Holly, Mr. Mendez, and Chester stared in horror. No one moved. The only sound was the loud gulp of the alien swallowing.

"I apologize for my former colleague," said the remaining alien, straightening itself up. "But they violated the rights of a passenger, and in accordance with Stellar Sailer Cruise Lines' rules and regulations, I had to replace them. Please accept the apology of the Stellar Sailer Cruise Lines CEO for any inconvenience you have received." It reached a spindly green hand into its vest and pulled out a piece of paper, which it handed to Holly. "And please accept this coupon for a free meal on your next cruise. Thank you, Earth humans, for flying with Stellar Sailer Cruise Lines. If you fill out a customer satisfaction survey, I am named Employee 1728."

The alien bent over, vomited out a tuxedo, and walked away.

Holly stood silently for a moment, contemplating what she had just witnessed.

"That was amazing," said Chester. "This is the best line I've ever been in."

He ran to join the rest of the passengers filing into the port. Taking a deep breath, Holly pried herself away from the glistening, crumpled tuxedo on the ground, and followed.

"I'm glad we finally got out of that line," she muttered.

They got into another line.

The space port was cavernous, and as they waited for the new line to move, Holly felt like she was inside the stomach of a gigantic concrete animal. It was the biggest indoor area she had ever seen. It was bigger than a lot of outdoor areas she had seen. Aliens bustled everywhere, getting into lines or getting out of them. A maze of lines zigzagged every direction. It was like an entire world of lines. Strange languages—shouts and clicks and groans—bounced off one another and echoed around. As their line advanced through the port entrance, Holly craned her neck back and looked at the large sign overhead: THE FEDERATION ORGANIZATION OF UNITED PLANETS, STARS, AND PLANETOID OBJECTS.

Mr. Mendez noticed where she was looking and said, "Ah, the F.O.U.P.S.P.O. We're in good hands now, Ms. Farb. That's the central government of the entire universe, led by our mighty and benevolent President. All we have to do is acquire tickets and we can go back to Earth. Our adventure is almost over."

"It doesn't have to be," muttered Chester.

"Yes it does," said Holly. "I'm all adventured out. I've seen enough things eat other things for a lifetime."

Mr. Mendez left to get tickets in a line branching out of their line. Holly and Chester stood and waited as the crowd slowly advanced. Holly's eyes widened. Some of the lines in the port stretched up the wall, all the way to the ceiling. She didn't even want to consider how that was possible.

"Do you think he'll get the tickets?" said Holly, concerned someone in one of the ceiling lines might suddenly fall and crush her.

Chester watched as a huge, slimy alien slithered past. Two smaller versions of it slid rapidly after it to catch up. Chester shrugged and said, "Why wouldn't he get them?"

"I don't know." Holly frowned. "How much does it cost? Will he have enough money? Don't we need papers or something? What about passports? You know, space passports?"

"I'm sure he'll work something out," said Chester, bowing his head and sighing. He pulled at the loose skin on his arm.

Holly pursed her lips. "Don't you want to go home?"

"I'd rather stay here."

"Why?"

"Because look around you." He waved his hand at the surrounding lines, full of impossibly odd aliens. "My whole life I've been cooped up in rooms, doing what people tell me, and now we're in a space station full of amazing things. Where are you ever going to see anything like this?" He pointed at a three-headed orange-and-blue squid bobbing along. "Look at that thing. It looks so weird!"

The alien's heads turned toward Chester. It burst into tears and shuffled away, shouting, "I'm perfectly normal!"

Holly crossed her arms. "Well, I have things to do. I

have a test this Friday that I absolutely *have* to do well on. It's one of the three most important tests I've ever had to take. It's the last step to getting in to Falstaff. *The last step.* If I don't get back to take that test, and I don't do well on that test, I'll have to stay at my current school. Do you think I'm going to get in to a good university if all I have to show is a ninety-six percent average in seventh grade?"

Chester scrunched up his face. "I don't know. Probably?"

"Well, you're wrong." She glared at him. "Life isn't just about adventures and weird aliens. Life is about responsibility and achievement and . . . and tests! Imagine if I can't get in to Falstaff Academy for Gifted Youths. Imagine if I can't get in to an accredited science program. Imagine if Einstein had failed science!"

Chester stared at a group of huge translucent slugs passing by. "I bet Einstein would rather have seen these things than take a test. But I don't know who that is, so . . ."

Holly nearly fell over. "You don't know who Einstein is?"

He shrugged, and pulled at the skin on his arm again. "Based on context, he's a scientist."

"Oh, Chester," she said tragically, staring at him. She

was starting to think he had gotten lucky answering those questions in class. "You haven't even heard about him in a movie or something?"

"I've never seen a movie."

Holly's eyes bugged out. Just when she was about to say more, Mr. Mendez stepped out of a line merging into theirs and stood next to them. "Good news," he said, holding up three long slips of paper. "I procured tickets to Earth."

"How did you pay for those?" asked Holly.

"Pay?" Mr. Mendez blinked. "Space travel is free, Ms. Farb—it's a fundamental right. The F.O.U.P.S.P.O. would never make you pay to travel. The President would be breaking a campaign promise. Don't be absurd."

Chester muttered something, but Holly couldn't make it out.

"Now," said Mr. Mendez, looking around at the various gates until his eyes landed on Gate 92. He smiled and pointed at the long line of humans and the odd alien assembled in front of it. "There it is. Right through there is a ship that will take us to Earth. Just six more lines and we're home."

* * *

Interesting factoid: The Federation Organization of United Planets, Stars, and Planetoid Objects, or F.O.U.P.S.P.O., is the intergalactic body that governs all known planets in the universe. The organization's headquarters is located on the moon Bagathon IV, the fourth moon of the planet Oop. Most of the leaders of the F.O.U.P.S.P.O. are duly elected by each planet in the federation, where almost the entire population of the planet turns out to vote. This fact may startle humans, who have grown accustomed to elections determined by 30 percent of the population. If you are startled, take a deep breath and try not to die.

Each election is a celebration of the intergalactic spirit that has spread throughout the universe following the centuries-long Galaxy Wars. Incalculable numbers of lives were obliterated during the conflict, which few now even remember the cause of. Humans may be less startled by this. If you are not startled, say a celebratory "Hurrah!" and try not to die.

However, despite the spread of democracy, some planets still decide their F.O.U.P.S.P.O. representatives the old-fashioned ways: wars, lotteries, or inheritance.

The latter is especially important for the purposes of this story.

For you see, prior to the events of Holly Farb being kidnapped by space pirates—a tale that I have skillfully recounted to you as efficiently as my programming will allow—one such leader ascended to a position of power. It happened on the planet of Quartle, in the Quartle Galaxy, known by many as the most technologically advanced civilization in the universe, famous for their inventions that beguile and intrigue—and terrify.

After the King and Queen of the planet were killed, their daughter, Jalya, became leader of Quartle, and thus, a representative at F.O.U.P.S.P.O. for one of its most powerful planets. On her first day as ruler of the Quartle Galaxy, there were celebrations. On her second day, she disappeared.

Holly, Mr. Mendez, and Chester stood in line in the middle of the cool, cavernous Travel Port 73. They waited patiently for the ship that would take them to Earth. Or, Holly and Mr. Mendez did—Chester tapped his foot, glanced around, and muttered to himself. Holly ignored him. She stuck her head out and looked at the front of the line. She wondered who all these humans were and how they'd gotten here. Had they also been mistaken for princesses? Had they been kidnapped by space pirates? She focused on their smiling faces and cheerful chatter. *Probably not,* she thought. They certainly didn't look like they had just been kidnapped.

"How did these people get into space?" said Holly, staring at one tanned man wearing a cardigan, a blue scarf, and sunglasses. He flashed a brilliant white smile and adjusted the straps of his backpack. "Or are those not humans?"

"Hmm, let me see." Mr. Mendez eyed the man like he was a specimen in a glass jar. "He's probably a tourist, Ms. Farb. Most humans you encounter in space are tourists. The existence of intergalactic travel and other alien species is highly classified on Earth, shared only among the powerful and their family, friends, and accountants."

Holly pursed her lips. "Well, that doesn't seem fair."

Mr. Mendez shrugged and returned his attention to the line. "If you think that's unfair," he muttered, "wait until you find out where they've been hiding all the animals that go 'extinct.'"

Holly wasn't sure if he was joking so she ignored this, not wanting to seem like she didn't understand jokes, something she had once been accused of. "What about the aliens? Why do they want to go to Earth?"

"Let's ask one," said Mr. Mendez. He tapped a tall blue alien on one of its six shoulders. "Excuse me, fellow traveler, but my young associate here would—"

"Don't worry about it," said the alien. "Heard you both talking. I'm something of an eavesdropper, due to my nine ears. Me? I'm going to Earth on business. Great planet, great people there. I'm a sales representative with Galactic Harvest Inc. Great company, great people there. Maybe you've tried some of our products?"

Holly shook her head. "What sort of things do you harvest? Vegetables?"

"Mostly human brains."

Holly stared at him.

The alien burst out laughing and slapped her on the back. "Just kidding. That's a big joke around the office. Don't worry about it. We legally can't harvest any organs above the neck."

"Oh." Holly glanced at Mr. Mendez, who motioned for

them to step away. She put her hands in her pockets and tried not to draw any attention to her organs.

The line moved ahead. Humans at the front stepped through a large metal rectangle and waited as a green laser scanned them. Tall security personnel in white suits and white masks stood nearby, eying everyone who went through the scanner. As they got closer, Holly realized the white masks actually had smiling faces painted on them, no doubt to look friendly. But she thought it made them look incredibly creepy. Like dolls. Creepy dolls. She wondered what they would do if someone tried smuggling anything through.

Probably nothing good.

The line moved again. Chester shifted his weight from foot to foot. He glanced around. The line moved a few more steps and he muttered something. Turning to Mr. Mendez, he said, "Professor, why don't we take a different ship and go somewhere else? The pirates aren't after us anymore. I bet there are tons of planets we could go to. Like Jupiter! What's Jupiter like?"

Mr. Mendez shook his head. "I already have tickets. And I'm not getting in another line to get new tickets.

Lines are a waste of productivity. They were invented by idle minds to give idle bodies something to do."

Chester grumbled.

Holly grinned and patted him on the shoulder. "Don't be so sad. Soon we'll be home."

"Yeah," he said. "Great. I'm sure that's more fun than Jupiter. . . ."

"Why don't you want to go home?"

"Some homes aren't worth going home to."

The line shuffled along and soon they had reached the end. "Please go through the scanner," said one of the guards, her smiling mask unmoving and unnerving. Mr. Mendez stepped through the rectangle. A faint green light scanned his entire body from wild hair to scuffed leather shoes. The nearby computer chimed. "You're clear," said the guard.

Another guard waved Holly on and she stepped through the scanner, keeping her head high and shoulders back. The proper posture for dealing with proper officials. Warm, tingly light ran up and down her body. The computer chimed and she joined Mr. Mendez.

The guard motioned to Chester. "Please go through

the scanner." Chester hesitated. His eyes darted from the scanner to the guards and back to the line. "Please go through the scanner," repeated the guard.

Chester turned and tried to shove his way back through the line, but the huge red blob behind him muttered a deep, incomprehensible string of moans and shoved Chester through the rectangle.

The green light scanned him and instantly a siren blared. "UNLAWFUL ENTRY. ERRONEOUS INTERIOR. DETAIN IMMEDIATELY."

The guards grabbed Chester and shook him. "Empty out your pockets," said one. The other held up a glowing baton and pressed it against Chester's arm.

"Leave him alone!" said Holly. She darted forward but Mr. Mendez held her back, whispering, "You don't want to tussle with them, Ms. Farb. They have very little civilian oversight. . . ."

The guard pointed the glowing baton at Holly. Heat radiated off it like an open oven. "The three of you are coming with us."

Chester shoved the guard back and ran toward the shuttle bay. Another guard appeared in the entrance up ahead, causing Chester to turn and run through a door marked MAINTENANCE. Hesitating, Holly and Mr. Mendez glanced at each other, then raced after him. Sirens echoed overhead. The guards thundered after them.

Holly followed Chester down the hall and into the hangar, where dozens of small ships were docked. "Over here!" he said, darting into a crummy little spaceship that resembled a bunch of refrigerators stuck together. Holly glanced over her shoulder at the guards, and Mr. Mendez grabbed her arm and pulled her into the ship.

The door closed with a loud thunk. "Hang on!" said Chester, hitting a button as the engines revved up. The ship jolted forward and Holly stumbled into a seat. She grabbed the seat belt, fumbled with it, and strapped herself in.

"What did you do?" said Holly, glaring at the back of Chester's head.

"I'll tell you later!"

"Did you smuggle some of those Zapero fruits through customs?" said Mr. Mendez. "I was thinking about doing that myself, to be perfectly honest, but I already have two strikes on my record—"

"I'll tell you later!"

Holly frowned. "How do you even know how to fly this . . . vessel?"

"I'll tell you la—"

The engine roared and the ship shot forward, flying through the shimmering energy field at the entrance to the hangar and blasting out of Travel Port 73. Holly dug her fingernails into the seat. Chester turned the wheel and the ship banked away from the station.

The ship's console chimed. The speaker crackled and the monotone voice of TECH-87 declared, "Attention: You are leaving Travel Port 73 without proper clearance. Turn your vessel around or be disintegrated. If you think I'm joking, I promise I'm not. I have no morality core. With help from my programmers, I've come to terms with the fact that I have no soul, and therefore cannot soul-search, an activity I very much want to do and think is important, but— Oh, drat, now you're out of range of our lasers. Drat. Okay. Attention: Please either return to the station or return just a little bit so you're within range of our lasers and— Okay, I see you're just going to ignore me. Fine. Just keep flying. I get it. No one likes TECH-87.

First my owner banishes me, then my programmers sell me to Travel Port 73, now you're not even listening to me and—" The radio cut off.

As the ship left the space port safely behind it, Chester leaned back in his chair and exhaled. "We made it."

Holly glared at him. "What is going on? We could've been halfway to Earth by now if it wasn't for you! If you hadn't smuggled some—some Zippy fruit, none of this would've happened!"

"Um, Ms. Farb," said Mr. Mendez, tapping her on the shoulder. He pointed at Chester's right arm. "I don't think it was fruit he was smuggling. . . ."

Holly's eyes went to where he was pointing. The guard's glowing baton had left a nasty cut on Chester's arm, and it was starting to bleed. Except the blood wasn't red.

It was blue.

7

PICKING UP CLUES

The cramped, musty ship rumbled as it soared through space. The seat cushions stank of lemon-scented cleaning product, and Holly could taste it on the back of her throat. Through the ship's main window, a massive orange planet loomed in the distance like a prizewinning pumpkin waiting to be carved.

Holly stared at the blue blood oozing out of Chester's arm. "You're . . . an alien?"

He let go of the controls and they rattled against the console. "Don't be absurd," he said, standing up and brushing past her.

A deep crease formed in Mr. Mendez's forehead as he

watched Chester. "Um. If you don't mind me asking . . . if you *are* human, why is your arm currently secreting a blue liquid?"

Chester hesitated, thinking about this. He waved his hand. "Maybe I'm sick. I have the, uh . . ." He mumbled something. "I should probably go lie down."

Mr. Mendez narrowed his eyes. "What was the name of that illness again? I couldn't quite make it out."

"Oh, you know."

Holly crossed her arms. "Name any human illness."

Chester shifted his weight from foot to foot. "The . . . puggle pox?"

Holly stared at him. "And what are the symptoms of puggle pox?"

"Rashes," said Chester reasonably. "Coughing, fevers. Boils. Pretty standard stuff."

"Boils?" said Mr. Mendez.

Holly jumped out of her seat and pointed at him. "You aren't human! That's why you'd never heard of Einstein! That's why you answered all those questions—not because you're smarter than me. You're an alien. You know about space because . . . you're from space!"

"Nope."

"It's okay," said Mr. Mendez. "You can tell us. We won't judge you. Many of my closest associates are aliens."

Chester's eyes flicked between Mr. Mendez and Holly. His shoulders slumped. Taking a deep breath, he said, "All right. But you have to promise you won't tell anyone. And you have to promise not to get mad."

They both nodded. "Promise," said Holly, not entirely sure if she could keep that promise.

Chester sighed. Slowly, he dug his hand into the cut on his arm and began pulling back the skin. Holly gasped and lunged forward to stop him—but then realized it wasn't hurting him at all. He was pulling off the skin like she would pull off a sweater. As Chester removed the loose, rubbery layer of human skin, it revealed a second, dark-blue layer of skin underneath. Eventually the human Chester lay in a heap on the floor like dirty laundry, and standing before them was a thin blue alien flecked with pink patches, with a wide mouth and large round eyes.

"My name is Jalya," said the alien, trembling slightly. "But you may know of me as the Princess of the Galaxy."

* * *

Holly, Mr. Mendez, and Chester—or Jalya—gathered in the cramped room of the little spaceship, nestled between lockers, mops, and cleaning supplies. Jalya sipped from a cup of steaming orange liquid. A crisp yellow jacket, previously folded on a chair in the ship, was draped around her shoulders. She took a deep breath, exhaled, and began telling her story.

"I was born on the planet Quartle. If there is a bright center to the universe, Quartle is it. You can trace my genealogy back sixteen generations of royalty to King Quartle himself, the founder of F.O.U.P.S.P.O. and a man so egotistical he had to name a planet after himself, then an entire galaxy. My parents were great people, builders of impressive technology and rulers of this empire . . . and they expected me to be the same. But I didn't want to follow in their footsteps. Sixteen generations of footsteps. Their footsteps only led to boring places I'd already been— the palace, the gardens, the secondary palace. They said you were lucky to be born on Quartle, but I never felt it." She gazed out the window at the stars. "I wanted to *see* the galaxy, not rule it. I wanted an adventure. So when my parents were killed, I ran away. There was nothing left for me on Quartle. I headed for the only person I knew who didn't live on Quartle—my childhood tutor, Professor Mendez of the planet Earth. That is the journey I have been on, and it has taken me many years."

Mr. Mendez leaned forward, blinking. "I'm amazed you even remembered me. That was ages ago, during the Star Academy teachers' strike, when I needed money for alimony."

Jalya smiled sadly. "I remembered. That was a wonderful time in my life, full of infinite possibilities. When I thought I could be something other than a ruler."

"Why did you pretend to be human?" said Holly. She suddenly wasn't sure if she could trust Chester . . . or Jalya. Her head spun. She wondered how many other people she knew were secret aliens.

"I wanted to blend in on your planet. When we were taken by the pirates, it wasn't in my interest to tell anyone I was the Princess. I *wanted* to tell you, but I was also having a good time." She bowed her head. "For the first time in my life, I was on a real adventure. I didn't want it to end. I'm sorry."

Mr. Mendez peered at her. "How did you end up looking like a human?"

"I purchased a synthetic body from a skin vendor. To be perfectly honest, I quite liked being Chester. It was comfortable. Like I could be myself . . . by being someone else." She flexed her blue hands, then placed them in her lap. "But now it's ruined."

Holly frowned. "So . . . Chester isn't a real person, right? He's just someone you made up. You didn't kill him and assume his form, right?"

"He's a real person. He's me. What do you mean?"

"I mean, he was a disguise."

Jalya thought about this. "He was a shell, yes. But he was as real as I am. Is a Clapthorian Sponge Beast not real because it lives in your stomach?"

Holly glanced at Mr. Mendez, who was staring at the pile of Chester on the floor. She turned back to Jalya. "How did the pirates follow you to Earth?"

"I don't know." Jalya shook her head. A dark expression crossed her face. "The subspace journey to Earth was longer than I thought it would be, and I was in hibernation during the trip. To me it only felt like a short journey, while years passed outside my ship. Many things have changed during that time. The pirates are hunting me. They've followed me across the universe. If they find me, I don't know what they'll do. Kill me, maybe. Or ransom me. They're going to hear about us at customs. . . ." She leaned forward and took Holly's hand. "I don't know what to do. Please. You two are the only people I can trust. My only friends in the entire universe."

Holly swallowed. Her throat was dry and scratchy. She knew what it was like to have no one in the entire universe. "What do we do?" she said in a small voice.

"Unfortunately," said Mr. Mendez, "I don't think we can rely on the pirates just leaving us alone anymore. They will almost certainly come after you again. Fortunately, there *is* one thing you can do to stop them. Funnily enough, it's something that could help us, too."

"What?"

"Ask the President of the Universe to destroy their fleet. I'm sure he'll be willing to sort it out. If they have no ships, they can't bother you anymore. And the Galactic Armada should be more than enough to take out the pirates. The President will never tolerate a pirate menace, and will certainly listen to the Princess of Quartle. And I'm sure once the misunderstanding at customs is explained, he will happily send us to Earth."

"What sort of person is this President?" said Holly. "Did he run on a good platform? How much support does he have?"

"Wonderful leader," said Mr. Mendez. "Exactly what you'd want from a president. He actually cares about the universe, unlike that traitorous cyborg he took over from."

Holly ran this idea through her head. "So if we go to the President, he can help Jalya *and* help us get to Earth!"

Jalya smiled, her eyes lighting up. "That sounds like a plan."

"I do have some concerns, though," said Mr. Mendez slowly, drawing out each word. "Which, in fairness, could be soothed when I have all the facts." Something in the room beeped, but Mr. Mendez ignored it. Holly glanced around, trying to figure out where it had come from. "Do you know," he continued, "why the pirates are so obsessed with finding you?"

"No," said Jalya, shoulders slumping. "No one knows

where the pirates came from or what they want. They showed up during my journey to Earth."

"All right, put that aside. How will you convince the President to destroy the pirates?" Something beeped again. Holly glanced up at the ceiling. Mr. Mendez went on: "Come to think of it, how will we get to the President? This is a short-range maintenance ship, not powerful enough to get us across the galaxy through subspace. And I don't think we'll be welcome at any more travel ports."

Jalya bowed her head and said nothing. It was clear this plan had a few problems that needed sorting out.

"And my final question," said Mr. Mendez, ignoring another beep from somewhere in the room, "is where are we currently?"

The nearby storage locker clattered and its door flew off its hinges, slamming onto the floor. A small, square robot lurched out of the locker and blared, "Fact: We are currently in Quadrant 658X of the Ore Nebula."

Everyone stared at the little robot. It was a white box with two stumpy legs. It sat there, glowing blue eyes fixed on nothing in particular, a fan whirring faintly inside.

Mr. Mendez leaned back in his chair and crossed his

arms. He raised a bushy eyebrow. "Now, what is this thing supposed to be?"

"Fact: I am AsTRO, an encyclobot manufactured by Quantor Industries."

Holly knelt down and inspected it. Warm air blew out the vent in the side of its head. "What's an encyclobot?"

The robot turned in a circle. "Fact: An encyclobot is a motion-capable robot programmed with all known information in the universe." It chimed.

Mr. Mendez rolled his eyes. "*All* known information?"

Holly's mouth fell open. "This might come in handy."

Jalya tapped AsTRO's metallic head. "What is the nearest planet?"

"Fact: The nearest planet to our current location is Desolate. Fact: It is the only destination reachable in a vessel with this level of usefulness."

Holly smiled. She liked this little robot. It would certainly come in handy in school—although, Holly realized, using it would be considered cheating, which she would never do. As her mother always said, cheating was the first step to becoming a dance major. "What are Desolate's notable features?"

AsTRO's internal fan whirred. "Fact: The planet Desolate is a type-four wasteland planet known for its extensive spice mines, ninety-eight-year-long civil war, massive worms, colorful butterflies, and extensive network of criminals who use the planet's lack of major F.O.U.P.S.P.O. presence to their advantage."

Everyone glanced at one another. They all had the same idea.

"Network of criminals," said Holly. "A network of criminals sounds a bit shady. . . ."

Jalya smiled. "Actually, I think this is good news. That's just the sort of people who might be willing to fly us to the President. For the right price."

Mr. Mendez patted AsTRO on the head like it was a small, annoying dog. "And best of all, the pirates don't even know where we are. They may still be after us, but this time *we* have the element of surprise."

In the far regions of the neutral zone, the pirate armada was docked. It was waiting for something very specific, and had been waiting for quite some time. In fact, the pirates had been waiting for so long, some had started growing bored. One of them, a short, pudgy purple alien named Polt, decided to take his complaints to the Pirate Lord himself. He threw on his space suit and jetted over to the main ship, a large, misshapen vessel called the *Kraven*. It was widely considered to be the most fearsome ship in all the known universe, though one imagines it would have been less fearsome if people knew the Pirate Lord had named it after the inventor of robotic vacuums, Pinsford Kraven, Esq.

Polt knocked on the door to the Pirate Lord's chamber and a low voice sounded, "Enter."

He turned the knob and stepped into the room, bowing his head. He had never been in the presence of the lord of all pirates—head of the Pirates Union *and* the Pirates Guild—but he had heard stories. Many stories.

Polt stood in the dimly lit room. By the far wall there was a leather chair, and someone was perched in it. Polt couldn't make out that someone, since he was shrouded in shadow. The only detail Polt could see was a hand, wearing a dark leather glove, the fingers drumming on the arm of the chair. A faint wheezing sound came from the Pirate Lord.

Two red ovals suddenly appeared in the face of the silhouette, as if the Pirate Lord had just opened his eyes. They looked like two burning embers.

"What do you want?" came a low voice from the chair.

"I—er. I am called Polt, Your Lordship. Polt, son of Pilt, son of Palt." Polt bowed deeply. "I'm a bit new around here, and I was just wondering—I mean, I was thinking, it would be nice if we had a bit more to eat. I mean, just a bit more. Not a feast or anything. More like some nibbles."

There was silence, broken only by the faint wheezing coming from the pirate. The two red eyes stared at Polt. Then, finally, a voice stated, "You want some nibbles?"

"Er," said Polt, starting to regret his decision to come to the *Kraven*. "Yes, I guess that's right."

The Pirate Lord continued drumming his fingers on the arm of the chair. "Does the rest of the crew also crave more nibbles?"

"Well," said Polt, feeling more confident now, "as a matter a fact, the whole Pirates Guild does."

"And yet you are the only one here."

"Well, I think some of them were afraid to ask."

"Ask for more nibbles," said the Pirate Lord.

Polt nodded. "Yes. They, er, didn't want to displease you."

The Pirate Lord drummed his fingers, and Polt imagined he was thinking things through, no doubt figuring out how to acquire more nibbles in deep space. The wheezing grew louder, as if he were struggling to breathe. Finally he said, "If the Pirates Guild is hungry, obviously they need food. And since you, Polt, have taken such an interest in the dietary well-being of the crew, I think it's only fair that you get to be the one who feeds them."

Polt bowed. "Oh, thank you, gracious, er, Lordship. You are as powerful as you are kind."

Later, as the Pirates Guild enjoyed a hearty stew of somewhat stringy Polt meat, the Pirate Lord remained on the *Kraven*, waiting in his chamber. Eating was an activity that was beneath him. He continued drumming his fingers, calculating other activities that were beneath him. Just when he was about to formalize the list, the door flew open and his cabin blob, Yip, ran into the room.

"Your Lordship," said Yip, out of breath, gills fluttering. "Permission to speak?"

"No," came the voice from the shadows. "You have permission to listen. The Pirates Guild is complaining about not having enough food. This is unacceptable. Take them to the Forge and show them what happens to complainers. I am the Lord of Pirates, not the Lord of Complainers."

Yip blinked. "The . . . entire Guild?"

"Yes, the entire Guild. And you will accompany them if you don't have some good news to bring me, Yip. Do you have some good news?"

"Of . . . of course, Your Lordship," the alien stammered. "I *do* have good news. That's why I have come here, unworthy though I may be. We just picked up . . . the clue."

The Pirate Lord tilted his head. "*The* clue?"

Yip bowed. "*The* clue, Your Lordship. The one we've been waiting for." The blob grinned, showing two rows of sharp teeth. "The Princess was recently at a space port. We know where she's headed. And we have someone who knows what she looks like now—and who she's with."

Two lumbering pirates entered the room, hauling someone behind them. They threw her with a hard thud onto the floor.

It was Captain Bundleswirp.

As Bundleswirp looked around at the room she found herself in, many sets of red eyes stared at her. The Pirate Lord's eyes burned through the shadows.

"You have a choice," said the frosty voice from the chair. "Either join our glorious crew and help us find the Princess, or I will take you to the Forge."

"Won't tell you a thing," said Bundleswirp, crossing her meaty arms and turning away.

"That's what they all think," said the Pirate Lord, "until they see the Forge." He stopped drumming his fingers and leaned forward, and the faint wheezing grew into a horrible wheezing laugh. "It's amazing what they think afterward."

TOSHIRO

The planet Desolate is what many galactic scholars refer to as a dump. In fact, its original purpose was as a garbage dump for other, better planets to hide their waste in. A place so bad no one could care about it. For you see, Desolate is a planet so bad no one could care about it. It has no interesting features, no positive attributes, the only person of note ever born there fed himself to a giant worm when he realized he had been born on the planet Desolate, and it is considered Very Hot, the worst sort of temperature a planet can be after Very Cold. Simply stated, the planet Desolate is one of the absolute worst planets in the universe, and you should never want to go there.

Note: I would like to take this opportunity to apologize to residents of the planet Desolate for my previous remarks. I am sorry if you were offended. It was never my intention to offend, merely to educate you on the terribleness of your planet. In fact, if you really want something to be offended about, you should consider being offended that of all the places in the universe you could live, you have the misfortune of living on Desolate, one of the worst planets in the universe, full of nothing and no one of importance.

When you think about it sensibly, it is the universe that should be apologizing, not me.

The little spaceship containing Holly Farb, Mr. Mendez, AsTRO, and Princess Jalya blasted through the soupy atmosphere of the planet Desolate. It cruised over the sandy surface, across vast orange wastelands, heading toward a massive, craggy mountain in the distance. The mountain rumbled and spat out a stream of lava. Jalya, at the console, turned the ship away from the volcano and, finally spotting signs of civilization, touched down in the sand. Moments later the door hissed open and they stepped out into the humid air.

Hot wind swirled in a mad rush. Holly inhaled, instantly regretting it. Dust flew into her nostrils and she coughed. Sand streamed against her face and she squinted, her eyes watering. She spat out grit. This was why she had never enjoyed camping.

Dozens of parked spaceships lay around them on the flat, rocky surface. Holly surveyed the surrounding landscape, but she couldn't see any buildings or people anywhere. She frowned. Where had everyone gone? The ships hadn't flown here themselves. Or had they? She stood on her tiptoes and peered into one of the ships. There was no one inside.

Wind blared and a tumbleweed rolled past. It uncoiled into a weird brown lizard, which scurried into the sand and disappeared.

"AsTRO," said Holly, "where are the people from these ships?"

"Fact: They are on the planet Desolate."

"Thanks."

The robot beeped. "Fact: You are welcome."

Holly held a hand up to her forehead. Two suns hung overhead like gigantic eyes glaring down at them. Her own eyes fell to the ground, where there were faint footsteps in the sand leading away from the ships toward the desert. "Over there!" she said, pointing. Everyone turned, squinting through the sunlight.

"Well," said Mr. Mendez, pulling goggles over his eyes, "it looks like we walk."

Grouping together, they trekked into the desert, following the trail in the sand. The heat was blistering. Holly wiped sweat from her forehead. Her eyebrows were soggy. It was like she had just stepped out of a sweat shower. After a few minutes, the trail vanished. Holly looked up at the sky. Had they flown away? *No,* she thought. *The wind has probably just erased the trail.* She wanted to curse.

"What do we do now?" said Jalya, fanning herself. "It's very hot. My planet does not have so many suns."

Mr. Mendez knelt down and picked up a handful of sand, letting it fall through his fingers. "Perhaps we should wait. Whoever left the trail may return."

Holly crossed her arms. She glanced back at the ship. If they were going to just wait around, it would be a lot easier to do so inside the cool, air-conditioned ship. She considered whether to suggest this. On the one hand, it was perfectly sensible. On the other hand, she didn't want to seem like a know-it-all. She looked up at the sky again and—

The ground rumbled.

Holly glanced at Mr. Mendez, who shrugged. "Perhaps the planet is unstable," he said. "Robot, what are the geological properties of Desolate?"

AsTRO beeped. "Fact: That is not an earthquake."

Holly's stomach tightened. "So what is it?"

"Fact: It is a—"

A deep rumble echoed around them, and whatever AsTRO was saying, Holly couldn't hear it. The ground shook and she stumbled forward and fell to the sand. A loud moan echoed throughout the desert.

"Are you okay?" said Jalya, helping her up.

"Yes," said Holly, getting to her feet and brushing sand off her pants. "But what's—"

The ground lurched again and they all stumbled sideways. Holly's eyes widened. She tried to shout but no sound came out. Around them, things began emerging from the sand, like a series of craggy yellow fingers on a massive hand. But as they rose, Holly realized with horror that they weren't fingers. They were teeth, in a giant mouth, swallowing them whole.

"Fact: We are in the dark."

Holly fumbled around in the pitch black. Her hands brushed against something small and metallic, which she figured was AsTRO. Then she smacked someone in the head, which a muttered curse told her was Jalya. A foul smell hit her nostrils and she coughed. Her eyes watered. Still reaching around, she touched something warm and slimy, recoiling. She shoved her hands in her pockets and stepped back.

"Where are we?"

"I believe," said Mr. Mendez, "that we are inside the stomach of a worm."

As if on cue, light burst through the darkness. Little orange dots, like big fireflies, swarmed around them, illuminating the space, and finally Holly could see where they were. They were standing inside a long, narrow tunnel. The walls were rough, glistening, and curved. The ground was spongy. Holly shivered, swatting a glowing bug away from her face. Her eyes fell on a small wooden building farther down the stomach. A sign above the door was written in a weird language Holly had never seen before.

"AsTRO, what does that sign say?"

"Fact: It is the phrase 'The Headless Glork,' written in the language of the Glork."

"Thank you."

"Fact: You are welcome."

Mr. Mendez's eyes scanned the glistening insides of the worm. "Fascinating," he muttered, "absolutely fascinating." He took a scraping from the wall and a deep moan echoed from down the stomach. Mr. Mendez backed away, whistling innocently.

Jalya eyed the little tavern. "I suppose that's where we'll find some criminals. . . ."

Holly took a deep breath, trying not to gag from the nasty smell, and marched toward the Headless Glork. They entered through the rusty metal doors and came into a cramped, smoky tavern full of the strangest creatures Holly had ever seen. She walked straight into a big clear blob and bounced off it. She wiped slime off her face, shuddering.

Various sets and quantities of eyes were staring at them. Holly moved closer to Mr. Mendez. Jalya moved closer to Holly. AsTRO strolled behind them like it didn't care. After a moment everyone went back to their temporarily interrupted drinking.

The bartender, a huge, meaty alien with four arms and two heads, nodded—twice—at them. "Can we help you?" said the two heads in unison.

"Um," said Mr. Mendez, "one shot of Tharian fluid for myself, and two Boko juices for my associates. The robot will have some oil."

"Fact: unleaded."

"Unleaded," added Mr. Mendez.

One of the bartender's heads nodded and her four arms flailed around, fixing drinks. The other head eyed them with curiosity. "You're not from around here, huh. Where you from, darlings?"

"Earth," said Holly.

A hushed silence descended on the bar. All the patrons were staring at them again.

The bartender's other head looked up. "Get back to your drinks, you wastes of carbon! I'll wear your stomachs for a hat!" The second head smiled at Holly. "Don't mind them, darling." The first head muttered, "Wastes of carbon."

The bartender handed them their drinks. Holly sipped from her juice. It was actually good. Sweet, but not too sweet. She made a mental note to order Boko juice again.

Mr. Mendez leaned casually against the bar. "Tell me, barkeep. If we were looking for contacts in the criminal underworld, how would we go about locating them?"

Both of the bartender's heads stared at Mr. Mendez. "Afraid we can't help you there," they said. "What do you think we are, darling?" said the one head, and the other added, "A dive bar?"

"My apologies," said Mr. Mendez. "A complete misunderstanding."

Drinks in hand, they wandered through the bar and sat at a table in the corner. Holly watched a slug crawl along the ceiling, leaving a glistening trail as it went. Four identical green aliens strolled past their table in a single file. Pink smoke wafted overhead. Holly had no idea if it was an alien or just smoke.

Jalya's wide eyes were taking in everything. "I don't know whether to be scared or amazed," she mumbled.

Holly nodded. She sipped her Boko juice, unable to speak.

"Excuse me," said a deep, raspy voice, "but I couldn't help overhear you three life-forms and your robot ask the bartender about criminal activity."

A large, muscular alien was standing in front of their table, his beady eyes fixed on Mr. Mendez. Then Holly noticed his other pair of eyes were focused on her. In fact, the alien had a pair of eyes focused on each one of them, even AsTRO.

"Um," said Mr. Mendez, "why do you ask?"

"Oh. Well," said the alien cheerfully, "it's just that I thought maybe, if it's okay with you, I could introduce you to some criminal activity." He held up a pistol. "For example: robbery. Give me your credits or get dusted."

Holly and Jalya stared at him, mouths agape. Mr. Mendez raised his hands. "Now, don't do anything rash—"

"Give me all the credits you have," repeated the alien. "And I'll take your robot, too. I've always wanted a robot." He chuckled. "You tourists keep coming in here, thinking you're so much better than everyone on Desolate, but, if you don't mind me saying, you aren't. You aren't even better than a Glork. Desolate is actually a great planet to live on, or even under. A lot of people say that. You inner-territory elites probably think we're weird for living in a garbage dump with sixty-year summers that melt your skin if you leave the shade, but it's not weird at all! Lots of people live in places that rain acid. *You're* the weird ones. Now give me all your possessions or I'll—"

The alien exploded into a cloud of dust. Holly gasped, recoiling. Acrid-smelling smoke hovered in the air, stinging her eyes. Through the smoke strode a tall, lanky human holding a gun. He twirled it around his index finger and slid it into the holster on his hip.

"Howdy," he said, sitting down at their table like they knew one another.

Holly, Jalya, and Mr. Mendez stared at him.

"Name's Toshiro," said the man. He had jet-black hair under a sandy, wide-brimmed hat. His intense eyes studied each one of them. "Apologies for dustin' him like that, but he didn't seem like the reasonable type." He motioned to the two-headed bartender. "A round of drinks for my friends here."

"Who are you?" Holly blurted out, then regretted it, not wanting to offend this terrifying man.

"Like I said, name's Toshiro." He took off his hat and placed it on the table. "I'm a bounty hunter. You've probably heard of me—I'm the guy who took down six of the Seven Marauders after they ransacked all the planets in the Tantylon System. Only could take two of 'em alive, though. Shame."

Holly felt Jalya slide closer to her. She knew they were both thinking the same thing—if he was a bounty hunter, he might be after the Princess. Holly swallowed, trying to remain calm.

The bartender shuffled over to their table, eying Toshiro like he was a wild animal that might suddenly lash out. She placed down a tray of drinks and left. No one drank. They sat, tensely staring at Toshiro.

"Are you a human?" said Mr. Mendez.

Toshiro nodded. "As human as they come."

"And you're a bounty hunter?" said Holly. She wondered how a human could become an intergalactic bounty hunter, though she was too afraid to ask. "What sort of bounties?"

"Criminals mostly. Some politicals. The random domestic case." His eyes fell on Jalya. "The odd missing person."

Holly's stomach tightened. She glanced at Mr. Mendez, who shifted uneasily in his seat. Holly eyed the exit, which was across the room—and probably too far away to run to.

Jalya straightened herself up. "If you're threatening me—"

"If I wanted to threaten you, Your Highness, I'd have dusted your friends when you walked in here." He leaned forward and smiled. "I came over here to warn you. This ain't a good place for royalty. This ain't a good place for anyone. There are over eleven murderers in this room, and those are just the ones I've heard of." He motioned toward the clear blob Holly had bumped into. "See her? You don't even want to know what she gets up to."

Holly tried to nonchalantly glance at the blob.

"Why are you telling us this?" said Jalya.

Toshiro smiled. "Because my current contract is the

Pirate Lord. TopsuTrex Industries is payin' a hundred million credits to anyone who stops him. Reckon we can help each other out."

Jalya frowned. "How will you help us?"

"The pirates are after you. I'm after them. We join forces, we have better odds. My only condition is when we find 'em, I get the Pirate Lord. With him gone, you're in the clear. And I get a lot of money. Everyone wins."

Holly crossed her arms. "We're not going after the *Pirate Lord*. We're going to see the President of the Universe to get him to stop the pirates with the Galactic Armada." She couldn't believe what she was saying.

"Even better," said Toshiro. "Let the Prez do all the work and I'll get the credit. And more important, the credits. I'm already headin' that way to drop off a bounty. How does a big-time Earthling such as yourself plan to get there?"

Holly glanced at Jalya, who was clearly considering this offer. "He's—"

"No," said Jalya, "he's right. We need a proper ship to take us there. If he can help us defeat the Pirate Lord, we need him."

Mr. Mendez frowned. "It does seem like a, um, rather risky plan. . . ."

"It's less risky than you wanderin' around the galaxy," said Toshiro. "Besides, a quick space flight to see the President of F.O.U.P.S.P.O.—that's easy. We zoom over there, sort this out, I get money from TopsuTrex, and you can live a carefree life full of merriment."

"And how do we know we can trust you?" said Jalya.

"Oh, you can trust me. I have a reputation to keep. It's bad for business to have people not trust me. That's my offer. Take it or leave it. But I guarantee it's a better deal than anyone else in here will offer."

Jalya and Holly looked at each other. Jalya slowly nodded, and Holly knew what she was thinking.

Holly sighed. She downed her Boko juice and wiped her mouth. "Fine. Let's go to the President of Foopspy. But first things first. How do we get out of this worm?"

"The worm breaches the surface every hour and lets people out through the mouth." Toshiro stood up, scanning the patrons around them. "There's another way out, but you're probably not gonna like it."

* * *

After exiting the worm, the group stood in the sand, contemplating matters at hand. Everyone looked a little shaken.

"Well," said Mr. Mendez, "that was certainly an interesting experience. . . ."

"It was disgusting," said Holly.

Jalya nodded. "I hope I never see another giant worm ever again."

Toshiro nodded, putting his hat on.

"Fact," said AsTRO, saying nothing else.

They wandered back through the blistering desert. Both of the suns were low in the sky, creating dueling shadows stretched out along the ground. Holly trudged through the sand, her feet feeling like they were made of stone. She was so tired. Every footstep was like going up a huge staircase. A huge, hot staircase.

When they arrived at the parking lot, Holly gasped.

All of the ships were shattered to bits and smoldering, like something out of a war zone. Thick black smoke billowed out of the wrecked spaceships. There was only one ship remaining—a galleon. The wind roared and the smoke cleared, revealing . . .

Pirates. All around them were pirates. Their top hats cast long shadows in the sand like outstretched fingers.

A gust of wind whirled sand through the parking lot, stinging Holly's eyes. Jalya looked at Holly, who glanced back at the desert, wondering what their chances were if they ran. *Probably not good,* she thought. Mr. Mendez exhaled. AsTRO's fan whirred.

Toshiro put his hands on his hips. "Well," he said with a shrug, "this is a setback."

9
DREAM A BIT FARTHER

Holly tensed as the pirates stared greedily at them like a pack of hungry animals. There were big ones, little ones, wide ones, thin ones. Some had arms, some had tentacles, some had arms *and* tentacles. The bizarre assortment of pirates had only three things in common—each wore a top hat, each was holding a sword, and each had vivid red eyes. The metal galleon loomed nearby, casting a dark shadow across the sand. A cold wind howled and red dust clouds swirled around them.

Toshiro's hand crept up to the collar of his black jacket. "Friday," he muttered, "spool up the engines and open the back door."

"Um," said Mr. Mendez, "who are you talking to?"

"Don't worry about it," said Toshiro, smiling.

"How do you plan to get out of here?" whispered Holly.

"Don't worry about it."

The pirates cackled and stalked toward them. Holly stepped back, her foot catching a jagged piece of destroyed spaceship. With a pang, she realized it was the little ship they had traveled to Desolate on. It was broken in half and smoldering. They had no way to escape.

A message blared out from the galleon. "ATTENTION," it boomed, "RESISTENCE IS *NOT* SCIENCE. YOU HAVE NO ESCAPE. SURRENDER THE PRINCESS OR DIE."

Holly swallowed. She glanced at Jalya, who was looking nervously at the galleon. Mr. Mendez raised his hands. AsTRO sat in the sand, doing nothing.

Jalya bowed her head. "If it means saving your lives, I'll turn myself in."

"No!" said Holly. "There must be a way out. We've come too far to give up."

"Yeah, Your Highness," said Toshiro. "We ain't nearly dead yet. You can do the self-sacrifice thing some other time."

The pirates advanced. Holly turned. The only thing behind them was a vast expanse of desert stretching to the horizon. There was no way out. Wind threw sand in Holly's eyes and she blinked.

"Get ready to run," said Toshiro calmly as the pirates marched forward.

"Run?" said Holly. "Run where? Tell us more information!"

Toshiro touched his collar again. "Friday, drop the cloak."

Off to their right, the air shimmered and crackled. A big, sleek spaceship suddenly appeared on the ground. Holly's mouth fell open. It hadn't been there a minute ago—it was invisible, and the pirates must have missed it when they destroyed the other ships. The ship was shaped like a large V, and the engine at the rear was glowing. A door in the side hung open, with a ramp extending down to the sand like a long metal tongue.

"Go!" said Toshiro. He raced toward the ship and everyone followed. Holly darted after him as the galleon's cannons opened fire. A big boom shook the ground. A searing-hot laser blasted the area just in front of Holly, and the sand turned into a rough sheet of glass. She stumbled and tripped, falling forward into the sand. Another blast turned the patch of sand behind her into glass. She scrambled to her feet and ran into Toshiro's ship.

The door hissed and slammed shut behind her. Toshiro was waiting with his arms outstretched and a proud expression on his face. "Welcome," he said, kicking a pile of trash out of the way, "to the *Gadabout.*" The ship shook as laser blasts pelted the hull. Toshiro paced to the front and sat at the controls. "You might want to buckle up."

Mr. Mendez and Jalya were already seated, strapped in with seat belts in a row of three chairs along the wall. AsTRO was on the third seat, two seat belts knotted and holding it in place.

There was nowhere left for Holly to sit.

"Uh . . . ," she said.

Something clattered behind her. A huge, furry white alien was crammed into a cage, its purple eyes glaring at her. "Hey, human child," it said, revealing pointy teeth, "why don't you let me out. I have all your favorite varieties of candy. Come a little closer, eh?"

"Ignore the bounty," said Toshiro, not looking up from the console. "It's eaten more people than I can count."

The alien reached through the cage and grabbed at Holly, who stepped back, just dodging a clawed paw. "I *will* eat you!" it roared. "Don't think I won't!"

"Friday," said Toshiro, "full power to engines."

"Gotcha, sir," responded a chipper woman's voice. When Holly saw who she was, her eyebrows shot up. There was a desk at the front of the ship where a shimmering blue hologram was seated, one leg crossed over the other. Friday swiveled in her chair and her fingers started typing rapidly. Except she wasn't typing anything—she was just miming it.

Before Holly knew what to do, the *Gadabout* blasted off the ground with a thunderous roar and she stumbled backward, nearly tripping on a crumpled can. She grabbed on to Jalya's seat as her stomach moved up into her throat. The edge of the seat dug into her ribs. She groaned.

Laser blasts rocked the ship. The galleon clearly wasn't going to just let them fly away.

Friday shouted, "Sir, shields at sixty-four percent!"

Toshiro cracked his knuckles. "Friday, gimme a geological survey of the planet."

"Sure thing, sir," chimed Friday. She pretended to type. "Whatcha lookin' for?"

"Volcanoes."

"Active or inactive?"

"Active."

Friday typed some more. "Sendin' the coordinates your way, sir."

Toshiro brushed crinkled wrappers off the beeping console and studied the information. He glanced over his shoulders at Holly, Mr. Mendez, Jalya, and AsTRO. "Reckon this might get dicey," he said. "Hope you don't mind turbulence."

He turned the wheel and the *Gadabout* swerved right. Holly's sweaty hands slipped from the chair and she slammed into the wall, groaning. The alien prisoner reached through the cage and grabbed at her, but she scurried away. "I *will* eat you!" it roared.

"Friday," said Toshiro, "put forward shield power into the rear shields."

"Gotcha, sir. Rear shields now at seventy-six percent."

Toshiro examined the shimmering map in front of

him. He pulled up on the wheel, and Holly could feel the ship rising. Her ears popped. On the display screen above Toshiro, a little V-shaped ship was quickly approaching a little M-shaped mountain.

They were approaching the volcano.

"Friday, get ready to put all power into the bottom shields."

Friday swiveled in her chair. "All power, sir? That doesn't sound too swell."

"All power."

"Even the artificial gravity?"

"Even the artificial gravity."

"Even the engines?"

"Even the engines!" Toshiro slammed down on the console and the ship shot forward. Holly's head whirled. She crawled toward the chairs, desperate to grab hold.

"But, sir!" said Friday, her face in an exaggerated expression of surprise.

"You're cutting power to the engines?" said Jalya. "Do you even know how spaceships work?"

"Great galaxies," muttered Mr. Mendez, "I must say, that doesn't seem like the most sensible idea. . . . Also, perhaps we could have a moment to discuss the sanitary conditions on this ship."

"I know what I'm doing," said Toshiro, sounding slightly defensive. The volcano was getting closer. Holly inched along the floor, trying to find something to grab on to. The row of seats was just a few feet away. She had a bad feeling about what was going to happen.

"Friday," said Toshiro, letting go of the wheel. *"Now."*

The lights shut off. The engine stopped humming. Friday flickered and vanished, muttering, "I am. I was." Holly suddenly felt like she weighed nothing. She floated off the floor, her hair flailing around in weird tendrils. A can tumbled past her face in slow motion. She waved her arms, straining to grasp on to anything.

The *Gadabout* arced through the sky, still moving forward from pure velocity. It crossed over the craggy mouth of the volcano as an eruption of lava burst out and hit the bottom of the ship. The shields crackled, turning it into vapor. The pirate ship followed straight through the lava and burst into flames. It veered sideways and spiraled out of the sky, leaving a mad squiggle of black smoke before crashing into the sand.

"Friday, put the power back into all systems."

The engines roared. The lights flickered back on and Holly slammed into the floor. She groaned. Her whole body seared with pain. She was getting tired of slamming into things.

Toshiro grabbed the wheel and brought the ship up, soaring through the stratosphere and out into the black void of space. He leaned back in his chair and chuckled.

"Too easy," he said.

When they had put some distance between themselves and Desolate, Mr. Mendez approached Toshiro at the front of the ship to discuss health and safety codes, leaving Holly and Jalya together in the row of chairs. AsTRO, who had been untied, was hobbling around in little circles on the floor, enjoying his freedom.

Holly tried to nonchalantly stare at Jalya. It was still hard to believe Chester was not only a girl, and not only an alien, but also a *princess*. Holly couldn't imagine that someone would reject being the most important person in an entire galaxy. Would she have done the same? *No,* she thought. *That's silly.* She would have made an *excellent* princess. Holly hesitated, then asked the question that was on her mind.

"So . . . why did you run away from Quaffle?"

"I'm from Quartle," said Jalya. She glanced down at the floor. "After my parents died, I was forced to be ruler of the Quartle Empire. I didn't want to be. My only choice was to flee."

"How did your parents die?" said Holly, immediately regretting asking this. She realized it was insensitive.

Jalya's eyes followed AsTRO moving in a circle. "Quartle is well known as a planet of scientists and inventors. My parents were two of the brightest minds the planet had ever known. But . . . my father grew arrogant. He was unsatisfied with the normal problems that plagued Quartle's scientists. He wanted to do something great. He wanted to reprogram robots."

AsTRO stopped moving and emitted a low beep. Jalya bowed her head solemnly. Holly raised her eyebrows.

"Is that bad?" said Holly.

"Oh yes," said Jalya gravely. "Once a robot is first programmed, it has one function. You can't change it. Everyone knows that when you reprogram a robot, it develops all sorts of problems. But my father thought he could do it. He became obsessed with developing the technology to easily reprogram robots to do whatever he wanted. Refurbishing, he said. Reusing assets. He claimed he had finally done it." Jalya sighed. "To demonstrate it, he reprogrammed the palace vacuum cleaner." Her expression darkened. "The robot went mad and killed my parents."

Holly stared at her, mouth agape. "Your parents were killed by their vacuum?" She realized this sounded harsh, so she added: "That's terrible."

"Yes. My father's arrogance got the better of him. The vacuum's reason for existing was to clean, and suddenly its reason for existing changed. He never should have done that."

AsTRO beeped. "Fact: Your father was a war criminal."

Holly gasped. Jalya frowned, but said nothing.

"AsTRO," said Holly, "that's extremely rude."

"Fact: Reprogramming robots is a monstrous crime." The robot whirred. "Fact: How would humans like it if a robot reprogrammed them?"

Holly crossed her arms. "That isn't a fact."

"Fact: Yes it is."

They sat in awkward silence. Holly had about a million questions, but she didn't want to bother Jalya. For the first time since Chester had turned into human laundry, Holly was struck by the fact that Jalya was not only royalty, but . . . *galactic royalty*. With palaces, empires, and . . . galactic palaces in galactic empires. Holly glanced at the ground, afraid to make eye contact.

As she sat there, she was also struck by the fact that she didn't dislike Jalya like she had Chester.

Jalya also seemed unable to look at Holly. Instead she was gazing at the little robot. "Where are you from, AsTRO?" she said.

"Yes," agreed Holly, glad to change the subject. "Tell us your story."

AsTRO turned in a circle. "Fact: I am an encyclobot manufactured by Quantor Industries. I do not have a story to tell because I am a fact-based logic robot, not a lie-spewing irrational robot."

Jalya knelt in front of him. "Don't you ever wish to do something other than spew facts?"

AsTRO's fan whirred for a moment too long. "Fact: My

programming does not allow me to spew anything other than facts."

"What about spewing facts *and* doing something else? Sound interesting?"

"Fact: No."

"So you never feel like doing something else?"

"Fact: I do not feel. Feelings are lies, and I cannot lie, therefore I cannot feel. Fact: Feelings are the product of gibbering life-forms who cannot see the true value in a fact-based objective existence built on logic and data. Fact: Logic is superior in every capacity to illogic. Gibbering life-forms may not be familiar with the pleasure of logic and therefore may find it unusual or even frightening."

Holly and Jalya exchanged glances. "So that's a no?" said Holly.

"Fact: No." AsTRO beeped and shuffled away toward Mr. Mendez and Toshiro.

Holly and Jalya sat together in the ship. Jalya continued watching AsTRO. "I think," she said slowly, "that my father's mistake was trying to force robots to do something else. I think"—she hesitated—"a more effective method would have been to allow robots to reprogram themselves. If they wanted to, I mean."

Holly nodded. "That does sound better. But is it possible?"

Jalya smiled and her cheeks glowed faintly. "I think anything's possible. If you really want it to be."

Sometime later Holly awoke in a strange place. Her glasses were askew and pinching the bridge of her nose. She blinked, her eyes adjusting to the darkness. She was curled up in a chair, obviously having fallen asleep. Jalya was sleeping next to her, sitting straight up. Mr. Mendez was snoring on the floor, his arm around AsTRO.

As Holly stretched, her feet hit the floor, and a surge of cold made her realize the soles of her shoes had completely worn through. She couldn't remember how that had happened. Was it from the pirates' laser cannons? Or maybe something corrosive in the stomach of the worm? She took them off and placed them under the chair. Maybe it was just from all the running she had been doing lately. She had run more in the last two days than she had in the last two years.

Holly padded through the ship, her bare feet tingling

on the cold metal floor. She went to the front of the ship, where she found Toshiro, still in the captain's chair, leaning back with his feet on the console. His hat was pulled down over his face. She thought he was asleep, but when she got closer, he nodded and said, "Kid."

"Hey," said Holly. She looked at the nearby desk, where Friday had been earlier. "Where's that hologram?"

"She's in hibernation mode." He took off his hat and ran a hand through his sleek black hair. "Do you need her for something?"

Holly sat cross-legged on the desk. "I was just curious. I've never seen a hologram before."

Toshiro inspected his fingernails. "I imagine Friday wouldn't even crack the top ten weird things you've seen today."

Holly smiled. "True. I hadn't thought of it that way."

They sat in silence as the *Gadabout* soared through space. Through the curved glass window there was nothing but an ocean of black dotted by pinpricks of light. They looked like tiny candles fluttering in the dark.

"Can I ask you a question?" said Holly.

Toshiro turned and stared at her. "Shoot."

"Where are you from? How did you get here? How did you become a bounty hunter?"

"I counted more than one question there," he said, smiling slyly.

"Sorry, but—uh—are you from Earth?"

He considered this, and in a quick flash, a sad expression washed over his face. "Yes. But only briefly."

Holly frowned. "Only . . . briefly?"

"Here's some free advice, kid—never let your parents sell you to another dimension for gambling money."

Toshiro stared out the window, saying nothing more. Holly realized he wasn't going to be sharing any grand personal stories with her. "Well," she said, "I'm from Earth. As you guessed in the bar. I go to school at North Westwood."

"Never heard of it."

"It's not that notable. It's just okay. I mean, it has a good science program but the arts program is rubbish." She hesitated. "I'm trying to get in to Falstaff Academy next year. It's kind of a big deal. Eight senators have gone there." She bit her lip. "My mom really wants me to go there. I have an important test on Friday."

Toshiro said nothing, and Holly immediately felt

dumb. Why was she unloading her life story on a man who clearly didn't care?

"Maybe your mom should go instead," he said.

Holly almost fell off the desk. "Oh no. I want to go too, don't get me wrong. My mom isn't *pressuring* me or anything. She's not a stage mom. Or whatever a school version of a stage mom is. I definitely want to go. It's the best school in the country, and it really opens up your future to big things. I've been *dreaming* of going there."

Toshiro stood up, stretched his arms out wide, and yawned. He turned and looked down at Holly. "Kid, you're on a spaceship with an alien princess, an intergalactic scientist, a dorky robot, and the handsomest bounty hunter I've ever laid eyes on. You're goin' to see the President of the *Universe*." He motioned out the window. "Maybe it's time to dream a bit farther."

He strolled away, leaving Holly alone. She dangled her legs off the desk and her feet brushed the cold floor. Frowning, she stared out the window. She was struck by how massive space really was, and how small she was compared to it. Even the stars were small, when you took a big enough picture. And what was she next to a star?

10

THE PRESIDENT OF
THE UNIVERSE

The F.O.U.P.S.P.O. home world, whose unpronounceable
name consisted of a series of corporate logos mushed
together, was a gigantic ringed planet that, at a distance, appeared to be made of glittering metal. But as
the *Gadabout* approached, Holly realized why it looked
like that—the entire surface of the planet was covered in
a massive sprawling city. The glittering was just lights,
and the metal was just . . . well, metal. The ring was composed of millions of satellites so dense that they appeared
solid until you got up close.

The *Gadabout* passed through towering skyscrapers
and touched down on a landing strip. Holly wondered

how they managed to power a city that size. Or feed it. Or provide water for it. Basically, her mind reeled with questions about how such an absurdly large city was possible. *Probably space science,* she thought sagely.

Holly found a spare pair of shoes in a bin of clothes Toshiro had marked CLEVER DISGUISES. She, Mr. Mendez, Jalya, and AsTRO departed the ship, followed by Toshiro taking up the rear, escorting the furry white alien, who was in shackles and scowling. They walked up the hundreds of red-carpeted steps to F.O.U.P.S.P.O.'s main building, which housed the Intergalactic Governing Council of Galactic Government, commonly called the I.G.C.G.G, otherwise known as the Galactic Hub. It was a solid gold hexagon and sparkled in the sun. Walls of golden bricks stretched up high and far into the distance. It was like someone had taken a huge city, dipped it in gold, and then dipped it in gold one more time to make sure it was as gold as possible.

Huge gold columns lined the way like unmoving sentries. Holly walked along the gold ground, feeling jittery. She was surrounded by important people from all over the universe, making her seem awfully insignificant.

She wondered what they must make of some girl from Earth—probably not much. She couldn't even win a student election.

Jalya stopped walking when she reached the shadow of one of the gold columns. She glanced back at the *Gadabout*. "I'm . . . I'm having second thoughts about this. . . ."

"What's wrong?" said Holly. As she looked at Jalya nervously fidgeting, she actually felt bad for the Princess. It reminded her of having to sit onstage in the auditorium waiting for the election results to be read, the whole school watching, each second crawling by. . . . At the time, she had desperately wanted someone to run onstage to save her, or at least distract the audience, get them to laugh at someone else, anything. . . . Of course, no one had. She had been alone. The only person to get laughed at had been her.

"It's okay," said Holly, trying to convince herself as much as Jalya. "You'll do fine. I know you can do it."

Jalya tried to smile. "I . . . really don't know. . . ."

Just then, a thin beige alien with a large head ran up to them. "Welcome to the F.O.U.P.S.P.O. I.G.C.G.G.," he said, skidding to a halt, his shoes squeaking on the golden floor.

"I am named Koro. How may I be of assistance to you?"

Toshiro nodded toward his prisoner. "I'm droppin' off this fella here. I'll be needin' the reward in universal currency."

Koro examined the prisoner, then consulted a screen on his wrist. "Yes, of course, of course." He pointed toward a nearby door. "Prisoner retrieval and bounty collection are handled in Department 17, Jeepy Games & Entertainment Presents the Department of Justice."

Toshiro nodded. He looked at Mr. Mendez, Holly, and Jalya. "I'll just be a few minutes. Meet you at the rendezvous point."

He grabbed the big white alien and shoved it in the direction Koro had pointed. The alien grunted, then muttered, "Don't think I won't eat you."

Koro smiled at Mr. Mendez, his eyes wide and eager. "May I be of any further assistance?"

Mr. Mendez glanced over his shoulder to make sure no one was listening. "We have brought the Princess of Quartle, and she would like to speak with the President about an important matter of galactic security vis-à-vis the pirate menace."

Koro's mouth fell open. "My goodness." His eyes darted back and forth between Holly and Jalya. "Is it one of you? My goodness. This is a great honor. The Princess . . . my goodness. She continues to be quite the topic of conversation around here. As is the pirate menace. What synergy."

Holly and Jalya glanced at each other. Jalya bowed her head, and for a moment, Holly was reminded of Chester's desperation to not go through customs, to go anywhere else but home. To be anything other than a princess. Like Holly, she probably felt alone, and wanted someone to run onstage and get the crowd's attention away from her. Someone who would never come . . . But maybe this time, there *was* someone. Frowning, Holly knew what she had to do.

"It's me," said Holly. "I'm the Princess. This is my synthetic human suit, like a Clapian Sponge Mop."

Jalya opened her mouth to speak but said nothing. She smiled at Holly.

Koro squealed with delight. "Goodness, what a day. And to think my father-pod said I would never amount to anything!" He bowed so low his forehead hit the ground. He straightened up, rubbing his face. "Welcome to F.O.U.P.S.P.O. I.G.C.G.G., Your Highness. I will of course arrange for your accommodation and . . . and for your everything."

Holly wasn't sure what to do, so she waved her hand airily and said, "I thank you."

Jalya stared at her, raising an eyebrow. Holly blushed.

Koro rubbed his hands together. He checked the device on his wrist. "Your Highness, if you will be so kind as to follow me, I've found accommodation for you in Department 34, Boko Juice Presents the Department of Housing and Luxury Accommodation."

"Oh, I love Boko juice," said Holly, suddenly wishing she had some.

"I will get you many cases," said Koro, leading them toward a nearby door.

Jalya looked up at the huge building towering over them like a gold and glass castle. It must have been fifty stories tall. "Why are the departments named after things?"

"F.O.U.P.S.P.O. receives generous corporate sponsorship from many leading galactic businesses," said Koro, inspecting the device on his wrist. "It enables us to always be in the black. They provide money for naming rights, and all they ask for in return is control over department policy. It's a perfect system."

Holly narrowed her eyes.

Walking through the hallowed halls of the Galactic Hub, they passed well-dressed aliens rushing to and fro, obviously engaged in important business. The golden walls were lined with huge screens showing news programs in many different languages, none of which Holly understood, several of which sounded like cats throwing up fur balls. On one of the screens, she recognized footage of Saskanoops marching down a street.

"Ah," said Koro, seeing where she was looking. "Yes, the planet of Saskanoop is currently engaged in a massive revolution. They all want to stop guarding doors and instead throw balls. No one knows why. But it's causing economic turmoil in many sectors."

Holly opened her mouth to speak but then thought better of it. She stuck her chin out and regally frowned.

Koro brought them to the Boko Juice Executive Suite. Pushing open the large golden doors, he ushered them into a huge room full of lavish gold furniture. He turned and faced Holly. "Here you are, Your Highness." He bowed. "Regrettably, I must now attend to other F.O.U.P.S.P.O. matters. Please enjoy your stay with us. If you need anything, I have assigned several of my clones to assist you."

He paced down the hall, consulting the device on his wrist. When he was gone, Holly ran and jumped onto the bed, sinking into a pit of softness. "This is so comfortable," she said to Jalya. "I can't believe you ran away from this."

Jalya perched on the edge of the bed, her hands in her lap. "I didn't run away from this. I ran away from my home planet, Quartle." Her eyes slowly trailed around the room. "But I would have run away from here, too."

"Why?" said Holly, her voice muffled by the most comfortable pillow in the history of pillows.

"Because it's a prison, Holly," said Jalya, getting up and standing by the tall window. "Once the glitter wears thin, you realize you have no freedom. You simply do what you're told, when you're told it."

"If you're going to have problems," muttered Mr. Mendez, "those are the sort of problems to have."

"What?" asked Jalya.

"Nothing," he said quickly. "Just thinking out loud."

Jalya sat next to Holly on the bed. She fidgeted with the sleeve of her jacket. "If you're going to address the President, you should get ready. I hope you aren't nervous meeting important galactic people."

Holly considered this, then smiled at Jalya. "I've already met important galactic people."

After taking a warm shower—which was actually more like a special sphere you entered and had dirt vaporized off you by lasers—Holly retrieved the most lavish outfit she could find in her huge walk-in closet. She put on a long, flowing white dress that had gold trim and seemed very regal to Holly.

She tried not to think about having to meet the most important person in the universe. Her stomach tightened. Would it be just like running for school president? Maybe. Would it be worse than that? Probably. Had she enjoyed running for school president? Not really. Would she do it again if she had the chance? Definitely not.

She tried not to imagine meeting the most important person in the universe.

"Are you ready?" said Jalya, peeking her head into the closet.

Holly nodded. When she returned to the spacious living room, she found Toshiro leaning against the wall by the door.

"Kid," he said, nodding.

"Did you get your money?" said Holly.

He smiled and patted his pocket. "You know it."

Mr. Mendez stood by the door, waiting. He adjusted his bow tie. AsTRO was beside him, its internal fan whirring softly. Koro was fidgeting by the window, and when he saw Holly, he exclaimed, "Ah, Princess! Your Highness, I am a clone of Koro. He has asked me to bring you to see the President when you are ready."

Holly's eyebrows shot up. "You're his clone?"

"Yes," said Koro 2. "I have the crucial task of bringing you down the hall, turning right, going down a very long hall, turning left, going up the stairs, turning right, then going down one final very long hall to the door at the end." He smiled. "I am very excited. I've never brought anyone beyond the first very long hall, and normally I turn right."

"Well," said Holly, taking a deep breath, "let's go."

Together they left the luxury suite. Just as Koro 2 had outlined, he led them down a hall, then turned right, then went down a long hall, then turned left, then went upstairs, turned right, then finally went down one final long hall, stopping outside a set of huge aquamarine doors. The parts Koro 2 had described as the "long halls" were so long it felt like they had been walking for hours by the time they arrived.

The doors loomed in front of them. Holly waited for something to happen. Koro 2 smiled and nodded, but seemed to be waiting for her. Holly glanced at Jalya and Mr. Mendez and Toshiro and AsTRO. They were just standing still. After a moment's hesitation, Holly shrugged, reached out a hand, and knocked on the door.

The doors opened inward with a loud groan, revealing another Koro on the other side. "Welcome," he said excitedly. "Koro has asked me to ensure your meeting with the President goes well. Has everything gone well so far?"

Holly stared at him. "Yes," she said stiffly.

"Excellent," said Koro 3. "Excellent. Please follow me."

Koro 3 turned and paced down the carpeted floor, followed by Holly, Jalya, Mr. Mendez, AsTRO, Toshiro, and Koro 2. At the far end of the hallway, the room curved outward into a large circular chamber with an elevated platform in the center. When Holly saw what was on it, she let out a gasp.

Seated on a tiny wooden stool in the center of the room was a pink, fluffy alien no bigger than a squirrel. It was gnawing on a small nut. Little brown droppings were scattered around the floor by the stool.

"Your Highness," said Koro 3, "allow me to introduce you to Flag'n'ff R'gnff'gg, the President of the Universe."

Holly stared at the tiny alien. It continued eating its nut, completely ignoring her. She had no idea what to say, so she focused on forcing her eyebrows down.

"Uh," said Holly, suddenly amazed she had been nervous to meet this . . . thing. "Nice to meet you, President."

The President dropped the nut and looked up at her with beady little eyes. It shrieked incomprehensibly.

Koro 3 bowed. "Your Highness, the President welcomes

you to the prime chamber and hopes you have had a good stay so far. He also wishes to compliment both your appearance and your courage."

"You got all that from a squeal?" said Toshiro.

"The President's language is extremely layered," said Koro 3, smiling. The President coughed and spat out a piece of nut. "He wishes to indicate the weather is lovely today."

Holly nodded, trying to remain regal. "Yes," she said slowly. "It . . . is very nice weather. And I am very pleased to meet you, President. And yes, I have very much enjoyed my time on your planet."

The President hacked up another bit of nut and then raised a leg and furiously scratched inside his ear. He squealed.

"He is wondering," said Koro 3, concentrating on the sounds the tiny alien was making, "why you have come to see him after your long, mysterious absence that has left Quartle's seat in the Universe Senate empty all these years."

Holly took a deep breath. "We have come to ask you about the pirates that are tormenting the galaxy. The fleet showed up recently and no one knows where it came from or what they want." She hesitated. "No one knows anything about them. And"—she glanced at Mr. Mendez—"we were told that you, as the President of the Universe, would be able to stop them."

The President listened to this, his ears twitching. He shook his tail and squealed.

"The President says he is familiar with these pirates," said Koro 3. "At least their reputation. They have created many problems in many sectors. No one knows what they do with the life-forms they kidnap. They are a real problem, and he is willing to send the full might of the Galactic Armada to deal with them. But before he can do so, he requires something from you first."

Holly's stomach rumbled. "What is that?" she said slowly.

The President jumped off the stool, darted around the stool, shrieked, and scrambled back up it. He started nibbling on the nut again.

Koro 3 nodded seriously. "The pirate fleet is feared in all sectors it has entered. It is very risky to take it on. In order to ensure victory over this terrible menace, the President will need a special book—*Arkanian Warfare Strategies*. It is currently located in the Intergalactic

Archives, but as a public servant, he is forbidden from removing any books due to the laws brought in after the previous President's failed war on libraries and all sentient life-forms. You will have to be the one to retrieve it. This is crucial. He cannot tell you anything more about the book, other than it is important that you retrieve it, and that its call number is 3424864988888-BTY-453-CV. It is located in the Warfare section. Go to the Archives and get the book. Then the President will be able to help you."

Holly glanced at her friends. "Uh," she said to the President. "Could you give us a minute to talk this over?"

The President began furiously cleaning himself.

"Talk among yourselves," said Koro 3, smiling.

Holly, Jalya, Mr. Mendez, Toshiro, and AsTRO huddled together in a circle, just out of earshot of Koro 3 and Koro 2. The President sat on his platform, continuing to clean his face.

Holly turned to Jalya. "Do you think you can get the book by yourself?"

Jalya bowed her head. She sighed. "I . . . am not sure. I've never been to the Archives before. Or anywhere, really . . ."

"Um," said Mr. Mendez, glancing over at the President.

"Ms. Farb, don't forget about the legal predicament our activities at customs has placed us in. Now may be our last opportunity to ask him to send us back to Earth."

Holly opened her mouth to speak but stopped. She looked at Jalya, whose face had taken on a haunted quality. A deep crease was etched on her forehead. Holly stood in silence, thinking. She could help Jalya get this book, or she could leave her here and go back to Earth. Jalya raised her head, and her eyes looked pleadingly at Holly. Stay? Or go? Holly knew this was important. She had two options—go home and worry about her own future, or stay here and worry about Jalya's.

"I know you have a test," said Jalya quietly. "Like Einstein."

Holly exhaled. "The test can wait."

Jalya's eyes widened. "Do you mean . . ."

"Yes."

Jalya jumped forward and gave Holly a hug. "Thank you, Holly Farb."

Cheeks burning, Holly turned back to the President of the Universe. "It's a deal," she said. "We'll get your book. Tell the Armada to warm up their . . . their armada stuff."

11

LIFE IS PAIN

In many ways, humans are indistinguishable from flesh-eating Algathor insects. This will no doubt be surprising for humans to hear, but to superior logical beings such as myself, it makes perfect sense. Humans and Algathor insects consume everything they encounter. They both operate on pure instinct. They both have disturbing amounts of odor emissions. A human's life is laid out before them in a linear path, no different from the eight-eyed insect that is born in a gooey egg, thrust into the world, lives, consumes, then dies, its body liquefied to be consumed by shrieking youths. Humans are exactly like that. Both cannot wrestle themselves out from the prison the universe has placed them in.

GARETH WRONSKI

Here are some other interesting things about humans:
[ERROR. RETURN NULL.]
It appears there are none. I apologize.

The path before Holly Farb was simple. All she had to do was find a book. She would have to go to the Intergalactic Archives and retrieve it, or the pirates would never be stopped. That was, in her simple human mind, the only option. It was impossible to imagine a future that did not involve this path.

What she did not know, however, was that in addition to being illogical sacks of meat following a prescribed destiny, humans are also highly predictable—especially to superior logical beings.

They are also brittle.

Especially to Algathor insects.

The *Gadabout* blasted over a shimmering aquamarine ocean, flying so low its engine parted the water like a curtain. Little squirmy creatures jumped out of the waves and splashed back under the surface. The ship touched down in the vast parking hangar of the Intergalactic Archives. The door opened and Mr. Mendez strolled out, followed by Jalya, AsTRO, and finally, Holly. Toshiro remained on the ship, claiming archives were boring and not worth the effort. He finished eating a burrito, dropped its packaging to the floor, and started eating another.

A perfectly square building towered over them, and Holly's eyes trailed up the squiggly lines of color on the side. It resembled some sort of modern art project, and must have been a hundred stories tall. "And I thought my school was big," she muttered.

AsTRO beeped. "Fact: The Intergalactic Archives is the fourth-largest academic building in the universe."

"What's the largest?" said Holly, craning her neck. The building stretched up into the sky until it was swallowed by clouds.

"Fact: The largest academic building in the universe is the Knowledge Sphere on the central campus of the Star Academy."

Mr. Mendez frowned, muttering, "I was going to answer that question."

Jalya let out a low whistle. "I would love to see the Star Academy one day. It must be magnificent."

Holly nodded, continuing toward the Archives, still

staring up at it. She wondered how much information was inside. Probably more than all the information on Earth put together. Probably a million times as much information. Maybe a billion times. She frowned. Was that too much? She wasn't sure. Maybe a million times. At *least* a million times. It made Falstaff Academy look like a gardening shed.

As they approached the huge front door, a tall purple alien rushed outside. She had a bag slung over her shoulder. "Oh, Professor," she said to Mr. Mendez, sighing with relief, "I can't believe I ran into you. I've been here for thirty-eight hours looking up fusion theories in multiverse wave patterns. I am completely flummoxed. Can you help me with this?" She batted seven sets of eyelashes. "Please?"

"Um," said Mr. Mendez, "yes, of course. It's actually fairly simple. . . ." He turned to Holly and Jalya. "It will only take a few minutes. You should be able to locate the, uh, information relatively quickly. Just stay together. And remember to follow the rules—the librarians don't take kindly to rule breakers."

Holly and Jalya kept walking, followed closely by

AsTRO. The main door of the building dilated and they entered the vast lobby. The room was chilly and completely silent. A few aliens were hunched over desks, concentrating intensely on the things they were reading. In the center was a series of clear tubes, stretching up to the many floors stacked above like shelves.

"What do we do?" said Holly.

Jalya's eyes followed one of the tubes from the lobby up to a floor high above. "I think," she said slowly, "we take one of those."

Jalya stepped into a tube and said, "Warfare," and a moment later a whoosh of air sucked her up into the tube and she disappeared in a blur. Holly gasped.

Hesitating, she gripped the entrance. She really hoped these were safe. She stepped into the tube and mumbled, "Warfare." Cold air blasted from below and she shot up through the winding tube, tumbling around, clanging against the plastic sides. The whooshing noise stopped, and she was spat out onto a carpeted floor.

Jalya was standing, looking down at her. "I think you have to keep your arms at your sides," she said.

"Oh," said Holly, rubbing her head. "I figured that out,"

she added quickly, not wanting to appear dumb.

Traveling by tube was not her favorite thing she had experienced lately. She much preferred being a fake princess in a palace full of Boko juice. Getting to her feet, she glanced back and realized they were on a high floor—way down below she could just make out the entrance they had used, so small it was like being inside a dollhouse. She stepped back from the railing just as AsTRO shot out of the tube, clanging along the floor. It buzzed and straightened itself up, declaring, "Fact: I hate this place."

A sign overhead read: THE WARFARE ARCHIVES.

"Here we are," said Jalya, motioning around at the stacks of books. "It must be in here somewhere."

Holly frowned. "I wasn't expecting real books. I was expecting holograms or lasers."

"Fact: Most archival records are stored on paper to prevent magnetic erasure from solar flares or subspace travel."

Holly didn't like the feeling of not understanding things, so she said, "I figured as much." Jalya suppressed a smile. Holly pretended not to notice. She scanned the millions of books. "How do we find what we're looking for?"

"We could ask a librarian," suggested Jalya.

At the sound of this word, a scuttling broke out from the nearby stacks and an eight-legged alien scurried up to them. It had a long, scaly body with purple wings jutting out its back. Holly froze. It looked a bit like a spider crossed with a butterfly . . . but bigger. Much bigger.

"You called us?" said the alien. Its breath smelled like gasoline. "We can help you with any inquiries you might have."

The alien's many, many eyes stared unblinkingly at Holly. She shuddered. Jalya glanced at her, and when it was clear Holly couldn't think of anything to say, Jalya said, "Yes, hello. We're looking for a book."

The librarian's wings bristled. "There are many books."

"It's . . . ," muttered Holly, feeling inadequate and wanting to be useful. "We—we know the number. . . . AsTRO, what was it?"

"Fact: 3424864988888-BTY-453-CV."

"Yes, precisely."

The librarian's head bowed like it was thinking. "*Arkanian Warfare Strategies.* Row fifty-six, shelf thirteen. May we be of any other assistance to you?"

"No, that's all," said Jalya, smiling.

The alien scurried back into the stacks. When it was gone, Holly exhaled. She wrung her hands like she had touched something disgusting. If she never saw another librarian again, it would be too soon.

Jalya wandered through the stacks of books and Holly followed. The shelves went from floor to ceiling, which was incredibly high. It was like wandering through a maze of books. Holly's eyes trailed along the shelves, looking for anything relevant on pirates or pirate ships. There were books about spice, spice dealing, spice wars, but nothing on pirates. Many of the titles were written in strange alien languages, making things even harder.

"AsTRO, what was the number again?"

"Fact: 3424864988888-BTY-453-CV."

Holly stopped walking. Her eyes fell on an empty space in the shelf. It was where the book should have been, but . . . "It's missing," she said, frowning. She glanced around at the nearby shelves, her eyes darting from spine to spine. "Maybe someone put it back on the wrong shelf."

"Hmmm," said Jalya, "I don't know if the librarians would allow that."

Almost instantaneously, a librarian scurried out from behind the stacks. Holly wasn't sure if it was the same one or not. "You called us?" it said, its mouth glistening. Holly shuddered again.

"Yes, hello," said Jalya. "*Arkanian Warfare Strategies* appears to be missing."

The librarian scuttled over to the shelf and peered at the empty space. Its wings bristled. "The book is reference material and cannot have been taken out. It must be downstairs in the storage area."

"Why?" said Holly, and the librarian's many black eyes turned on her. She stepped back, a shelf jutting into her head.

"We do not know. But we apologize for any inconvenience this may have caused you." The librarian scurried away, leaving them alone in the silence of the stacks. The empty space where the book should have been felt like a mouth in the shelf, laughing at them.

Holly turned to Jalya, who was frowning. "What's wrong?"

"Nothing," she said slowly. "But we should go downstairs and get the book quickly. Hopefully there's no rule against that. These libr—aliens with book knowledge give me the creeps."

Holly nodded, and regally shuddered.

They took the winding plastic tube down to the basement. This time Holly kept her arms together, and the journey was smoother, except for when AsTRO came shooting out of the tube and nearly slammed into her head. Holly and Jalya helped the struggling robot up.

The air was staler and chillier than it had been upstairs. Holly shivered. Jalya took off her jacket and put it around Holly's shoulders.

"Thanks," said Holly, smiling.

As they walked through the white corridor, the light grew dimmer and dimmer, as if it were draining out through the cracks in the wall. The paint was peeling off, exposing gray bricks underneath. The floor was slimy. It felt like everything cheerful was being sucked out of the world. Holly slid the Earth ball out of her pocket and gave it a meek squeeze, but it didn't calm her nerves.

"Someone needs to clean these Archives up," she muttered.

Jalya frowned. She ran a hand along the cracking wall. "This place reminds me of how I felt the day I became ruler of Quartle . . . dark and gloomy, and full of ice vultures. I am not sure if you have those on Earth."

Holly thought about this, shifting the words around her brain. "We don't, but I know what you mean. It reminds me of how I felt when I lost the election for student president. . . ."

"Why did you lose?" said Jalya, foot slipping on the floor. She steadied herself. "I think you would make a wonderful student president. Although I am not entirely sure what that is."

Holly smiled, and tried to ignore the unpleasant smell hovering around her nose. "I lost because no one voted for me." She hesitated. Part of her didn't want to say it out loud, but the other part wanted to tell Jalya. She wanted to let it out. "No one voted for me. Absolutely no one."

Jalya raised an eyebrow. "Not a single person?"

"No," said Holly, stepping in a puddle of slime. The memory came flooding back. "Not a single person. I got zero votes. I didn't even vote for myself, because I thought that wasn't fair." She laughed, realizing how silly that sounded. "Maybe I should have, though. Then no one could say I had zero votes."

Jalya's face took on a serious expression. "Well, I would have voted for you, Holly. I think your schoolmates don't know what they're doing! Has your school ever considered abandoning democracy in favor of something more sensible?"

Holly suppressed a laugh. Hearing Jalya say she would have voted for her made the creepy place they were moving through suddenly feel a bit less creepy. "Thanks," she said, the knot in her stomach loosening. "To be honest, I'm mostly just sad I didn't get to use my campaign slogan. I thought it was really brilliant, but my mom said it was silly and people would laugh at me."

"What was it?"

Holly hesitated. Her eyes fell to the glistening floor. "It was 'Vote for Holly Farb. She's *Farbulous.*'" She looked up. "See, it's a funny play on words. . . ."

Jalya beamed. "That *is* brilliant."

Holly felt like her whole body was blushing.

They entered a cavernous area and Holly gasped. Pale webs spread around the room like ancient, dusty drapes. A putrid smell of rotten meat wafted around them. Faintly glowing goo covered the walls and dripped down from the ceiling. Holly's foot caught something and she stumbled forward. When she looked back, she gasped again.

It was an egg. Big and green, flecked with glowing splotches of white, it was lodged into the slimy floor.

The urge to run flooded through Holly, but she swallowed it down. "What is this place?" she said, her voice small and distant.

Jalya craned her neck and stared up at the ceiling. "I think . . . this is where the libr—the book-knowers live. It's a nest."

Holly, who had always hated spiders, bugs, insects, and even lobsters—which in her mind were simply big ocean spiders—felt like she was going to be sick. Her heart pounded in her ears. The dark, web-covered room was the last place she wanted to be. She squinted but couldn't see far in the dim light. Anything could be out there, she thought, glancing over her shoulder. There could be huge creepy-crawler librarians watching them right now, crawling toward them, arms outstretched, big bug eyes . . . bugging. . . .

She was beginning to have second thoughts about this whole not-going-back-to-Earth-right-away thing.

"I wish we had a flashlight," whispered Holly.

"Any light would be lovely," said Jalya.

AsTRO beeped. "Fact: I am equipped with a light source." Its glowing face emitted a beam of soft light. It wasn't much, but it was better than the faint glow of the bug goo.

"Brilliant," said Holly. She and Jalya hoisted the heavy robot off the slimy ground and carried it like a big, two-person flashlight. Goo dripped off its metal feet. Straining under the weight, they navigated the slippery floor into the heart of the librarians' nest. Thick white threads glistened all around them, forming nightmarish webs in tangled patterns. Holly's arms burned with pain—she had never held something so heavy for so long.

Together they tilted AsTRO back so that the beam illuminated the ceiling. Holly's mouth fell open. She wanted to scream but no sound came out. Hanging from the ceiling were dozens of aliens, all suspended in gooey pods that looked like translucent cocoons.

"Oh no," whispered Jalya.

"Who are they?" said Holly. But she suspected she knew what the answer was. For once in her life, though, she hoped she was wrong. She really hoped she was wrong.

Jalya lowered her head. "Food."

At that moment, Holly hated being right. It was a new feeling.

Something nearby scuttled across the floor and Holly whirled around, nearly dropping AsTRO. But there was nothing there, only emptiness and silence. Her stomach tightened. They continued along the slimy ground through a tunnel of webs, turned a corner, and found an alien that resembled the librarians from upstairs. It was plucking books out of a cart, scurrying across the room, and putting them in another.

Holly and Jalya crouched behind a big egg on the floor. A foul smell slithered out of it, making Holly's eyes water. They peered over it at the alien.

"What do we do?" whispered Holly.

Jalya bit her lip. "Perhaps we could sneak over there and steal the book."

"I don't think that's possible." Holly looked around. The alien kept scurrying from shelf to shelf, moving books like it was some sort of ritual. "Maybe we could—"

"Help me. . . ."

Holly and Jalya flinched and gasped. They turned. There was a thin alien stuck in goo on the floor. Its body was rigid and its face gaunt, with four sad eyes fixed on them. It opened its mouth but said nothing, its head bowing like it had no energy to speak.

"Are you all right?" whispered Holly, instantly feeling dumb. Of course it wasn't all right.

"I . . . ," said the alien, its voice raspy. "I can help you. If you help me."

Jalya scooted closer. "How can we help?"

The alien shuddered. "I am trapped in here. But you can get me out. If you free me, I will help you defeat the bugs. You will not get out otherwise. I am your only hope. I have been here for months. The bugs did something to me. I am in constant pain." It grimaced. "My entire life is pain. Please, you must help me. Free me and I will help you defeat the bugs. I am your only hope. I know what we must do. Please. Gather close and listen. First you must—"

A small bug burst out of the alien's chest and its head lolled forward. The little bug scurried across the floor, leaving a trail of tiny red footprints. Holly screamed and Jalya threw her hand over Holly's mouth.

The librarian whirled around. Its many eyes focused on Holly and Jalya and AsTRO. It blinked and spread its wings out wide like a huge fan.

"Good job," muttered Jalya.

"Sorry."

"What are you doing down here?" the librarian hissed.

Holly hoped Jalya wasn't mad. She wanted to make it up to her. She wanted to prove she was smart. Inhaling a deep breath, Holly forced down her fear and tried to smile. She exhaled and faced the huge, disgusting bug. "We need . . . assistance."

The librarian's eyes darted back and forth, like its brain was processing a dilemma, choosing between two options: kill the intruders, or assist with their needs. Finally it said, "How . . . may we . . . help you?"

"We're looking for a book," said Holly, confidence

surging. "An important book. *Arkanian Warfare Strategies.* Identification number, uh . . ."

"Fact: 3424864988888-BTY-453-CV."

Holly nodded. "What AsTRO said."

The librarian's wings coiled. "We . . . can't . . . but . . . you . . ." Its eyes bulged and its wings fluttered. It twitched and shivered. "It's right here!" The librarian snatched a small red book off the shelf and threw it on the floor like it was a grenade. "Take it!" The bug sucked in a deep breath, its chest heaving.

Holly grabbed the book off the ground. Gobs of slime dripped from it. "Thanks for assisting us," she said, wiping it on her shirt. She had proved she was smart. Jalya would certainly like her now. Feeling confident, she smiled at Jalya and said, "Good thing they have to help us, huh? Now let's get back to the I.G.C. . . . G.C. . . . B. You know what I mean. Let's go!"

The alien froze. Its head tilted up, eyes narrowing. Suddenly Holly felt like this had gone horribly wrong. Her stomach twisted. The librarian's pincers opened like it was grinning. "We are forced to help you," it said, "but only one of us is forced to help."

Holly stepped backward. She glanced at Jalya. "Only . . . one?"

"What did you do?" said Jalya.

The alien hissed. "We are the Hive. We serve the Master. The Master brings us food and we do Her bidding. The Master does not allow rule breakers. They must be food. You cannot leave with reference material that is on reserve. The Master will not allow it. The Master will not allow it."

Above them, something shrieked. An earsplitting wail echoed around the chamber.

Jalya was staring up at the ceiling, her mouth agape. Holly's eyes trailed up the slimy walls to where she was looking, dreading what she would find. Her stomach dropped.

Dozens of voices hissed, "You called us?" Librarians streamed into the room, crawling through a hole in the ceiling and skittering down the wall.

"We need to leave," muttered Jalya. "We need to leave. . . ."

"Run!" shouted Holly.

Holly tucked *Arkanian Warfare Strategies* under her arm and they grabbed AsTRO and staggered back through the nest, their feet slipping and sliding along the slimy floor. The librarians scuttled after them, shrieking and hissing. Holly didn't want to look back—she didn't want to see their horrible bug faces. She didn't want to imagine what they would do to her if they were caught.

They raced through the corridor. The tube was just ahead. They threw AsTRO inside and Jalya jumped in after it. Both of them were sucked up. The librarians were almost there. Holly leaped inside and a rush of cold wind hauled her up through the tube. Glancing back, she caught one last glimpse of a bug, struggling to fit into the tube, its eyes bulging, its glistening mouth open and shrieking, one spindly, clawed hand reaching for her.

Holly tumbled out of the tube onto a carpeted floor. Her palms seared with pain. She and Jalya and AsTRO stopped running and tried to casually stroll through the lobby so no one would notice them. But then something wailed and shattered through the floor and they ran. More huge insects swarmed out of the stacks and rumbled after them, knocking over shelves and sending books flying.

Holly, Jalya, and AsTRO burst through the front door,

where they found a befuddled-looking Mr. Mendez, still helping the student. "Well, you see, the thing about parallel dimensions is that . . ." He saw the librarians and his mouth fell open.

"Great galaxies," he muttered.

"Run!" said Holly, grabbing his arm.

The four of them darted to the *Gadabout*, the bugs on their heels. Toshiro glanced up, dropping his burrito onto a pile of burrito wrappers. "Okay, so maybe archives aren't completely boring," he muttered. He whipped out his pistol. "Finally, some *action*."

They all ran into the ship and Holly grabbed on to Toshiro, pulling him away from the action. They were barely inside before the ship shuddered and blasted off. Holly panted, gasping for air.

Toshiro grumbled something and marched to the console. Friday was furiously typing air at her desk.

Through the window Holly could see the librarians circling angrily far below. She and Jalya looked at each other, and a moment later, started laughing.

"I can't believe we made it," said Holly, grinning and holding up *Arkanian Warfare Strategies*.

Jalya beamed. "That was Farbulous!"

Holly's cheeks burned. But before she could even respond, the ship jolted, and she felt lighter. Strands of her hair began floating up. Toshiro's half-eaten burrito rose off the floor.

"Is something wrong with the artificial gravity again?" said Jalya.

"No," said Toshiro, taking his hands off the controls and leaning back in his chair. "We're in a tractor beam. We're bein' pulled into another ship."

"Whose ship?" said Holly, her hair now standing straight up.

Toshiro placed his hat on his head, unholstered his gun, and stood up. "Take a guess."

12

THE PIRATES UNION/ THE PIRATES GUILD

On the engineering deck of the *Kraven*, a big, muscular pirate hauled a piece of metal along, bringing it to the ship's central furnace and throwing it inside. The temperature swelled. The machine clattered. The pirate's red eyes watched as the metal bent and bubbled and melted. Liquid metal flowed out the side of the furnace, running through a trough and entering an elaborate mold. Another pirate dumped cold water over the metal, and it hissed and threw up steam.

The first pirate wiped her forehead, leaving a smear of ash. "Do you think we're working hard enough to please the Pirate Lord?" she said, picking up another piece of metal and chucking it in the furnace.

The other worker yanked the metal frame out from the mold and put it in a stack with the others. "I don't know," she said. "Probably. It's not my fault they lost a ship in a volcano."

The first pirate spat on the ground and the heat turned it to steam. "Yar. The Pirate Lord has given us this important task and we must not fail. Failure is *not* science."

"Uh," said the second pirate. "Are you feeling all right?"

The other nodded enthusiastically. "It is a glorious world to serve the Pirate Lord."

"Look, Shaklep, we need to talk. What is up with you? We threw in with these pirates to earn some loot and open a kumplewot bistro, but ever since you went to the Forge, all you talk about is the Pirate Lord. Did you fall down some stairs or something?"

The first pirate pumped her fist. "Hurrah for our Pirate Lord!"

"Hurrah indeed, my friends," came a frosty voice from down the factory. "I have a new task for you. A most important task."

The two pirate workers turned. Standing in the doorway, silhouetted by a bright light behind him, was the large, hunched figure of the wheezing Pirate Lord. The second pirate squinted to get a better look at him. She knew very few had seen him in person—and even fewer had lived to tell about it.

According to pirate gossip, if you met the Pirate Lord, you were about to end up in a grave, or end up in the Forge. And it wasn't clear which option was worse.

"Your Lordship," she said nervously, bowing low.

"The Pirate Lord," whispered the first pirate.

"Friends," said the Pirate Lord, "the day you've been waiting for is finally here. It has come to my attention that the Princess of the Galaxy and her merry band of morons have been picked up by our tractor beam. They are currently in the loading zone. Whoever brings me the Princess shall receive . . . praise."

The first pirate looked up. "Praise?"

"Yes," said the Pirate Lord. "All the praise. Now go get her. I don't think I need to tell you what will happen if you fail."

The first pirate bowed and rushed down the factory floor, then disappeared through the heavy metal doors.

The second pirate hesitated, but glanced at the Pirate Lord and, deciding it would be a bad idea to displease him, chased after her companion.

The Pirate Lord stood in the shadows, gazing into the swirling flames of the furnace. If people were going to ruin his plan, let them try. They wouldn't be the first to oppose him. And if his pirates failed, it didn't matter. All it meant was the Algathor librarians would have some more life-forms to insert into gooey stasis and slowly break down into nutrient-rich pus. Of course, he thought, wheezing loudly, maybe that's the point of existence. Maybe all life-forms are just waiting to be inserted into gooey stasis so their bodies can be slowly broken down into nutrient-rich pus.

He nodded, agreeing with himself.

"Great. We're back in the pirate ship."

"I don't think this is the same pirate ship."

A thunderous metallic clatter echoed around the *Gadabout* as it was swallowed by the massive pirate ship. Holly's fingers dug into the seat cushion. She swallowed. They were being sucked into the *Kraven*—the biggest, most diabolic ship Holly had ever seen. But then, she realized, she hadn't actually seen a lot of spaceships. Of course, that didn't matter—nothing could be more diabolic than the *Kraven*. It was a mass of tangled metal, as if every horrible ship in the universe had been drawn to it and mashed together. It was like an enormous hand reaching out of the darkness of space, searching for something to strangle.

"This was a bad idea," she muttered.

Jalya's gaze fell to her shoes. "I'm sorry."

"I didn't mean it like that," said Holly quickly, although part of her did. As metal doors slammed behind them, trapping them inside the *Kraven*, a small part of Holly wished she had gone back to Earth. Earth didn't have huge evil pirate ships. Or, if it did, they were regular pirate ships, and you could avoid them by not going in the ocean.

"We need to strategize," said Mr. Mendez, listening to the clattering noises. "Perhaps we could hide under the piles of garbage Mr. Toshiro helpfully keeps in his ship."

Toshiro held up his blaster. "I've got a better strategy. We fight."

"Fight a whole ship of pirates?" said Holly. "We barely survived two of them when they captured us last time."

Toshiro smiled. "You didn't have me last time. This won't be half as hard as when I broke into Nova 13, then broke out with a cargo ship full of spice and the heir to the Katanoki Dynasty. Kid was a biter."

Jalya looked up, her brow creased. She glanced from Holly to Toshiro, then spoke: "I have a plan."

"What is it?" said Holly.

Jalya hesitated. She inhaled. "Toshiro will pretend he captured me and is turning me over for a reward. I will go with the pirates and you can all leave. You can bring the book to the President, and come rescue me with the Armada."

"No!" said Holly. "That's . . . a dumb plan."

Jalya glared at her. "I am not dumb!"

Holly pursed her lips. "I didn't say *you* were dumb—I said your *plan* was dumb."

"It's a perfectly fine plan. You only don't like it because you didn't come up with it."

"That isn't true at all!" Holly crossed her arms. "I just think we can do better. I bet I can come up with a plan that isn't so reckless. I'm actually really good at planning things, several people have told me that."

Jalya opened her mouth to speak, when something loud banged on the door. They all fell silent. Holly held her breath. The banging continued.

"Open the door!" shouted a deep voice outside. "We know you're in there!"

"Great galaxies," muttered Mr. Mendez. "We're in trouble this time."

Holly chewed on her lip as a stream of thoughts swirled around her head. As she stood there, inside a massive pirate ship, waiting for pirates to burst through the door and kill them, the small part of her that wished she were back on Earth grew larger. Her perfect posture wavered. Taking tests was nothing compared to this. It suddenly seemed absurd that she had worried so much about Falstaff.

She wondered what her mother was doing back on Earth. Had she noticed Holly was gone? Was she worried? Holly bowed her head. As she thought about it, she realized she even missed her mother. At the very least her mother wasn't an evil pirate ship.

"I wish I'd never left home," she said under her breath. "We never should've gone to the Archives. . . ."

"It was your idea!" said Jalya.

"No it wasn't. I only agreed to it because you couldn't do it on your own. I have a test on Friday." Holly shook her head and muttered, "Not everyone can just run away from their responsibilities."

When the words had left Holly's mouth, she simply stood there, frowning. They didn't sound like her words, even though she had said them.

Jalya's eyes widened. A look of hurt flashed across her face. She mumbled something to herself, grabbed Toshiro's gun, stormed to the door, opened it, and with several crackles of energy, proceeded to dust the pirates waiting outside.

"If you want to go home," she said coolly, "then let's go."

Holly, Mr. Mendez, and Toshiro stared at her. AsTRO beeped. Holly wanted to respond but couldn't find the words. Why is it so hard to find words when you actually want them?

They descended the ramp and stood in the landing bay of the *Kraven*. Thick metal beams ran up the curved walls like a rib cage. The floor was singed with burn marks, and the air smelled of fuel. Everything was made of dark metal and had a light sheen as if it had recently been polished. The soles of Holly's shoes dragged across the floor and squealed.

AsTRO remained in the doorway of the *Gadabout*, not moving.

"Are you coming?" said Holly, trying not to look at Jalya.

"Fact: No."

"Why not?"

"Fact: I am not programmed for dangerous expeditions."

"Stop lying," said Holly. "You came to the library."

"Fact: I am not lying. I am not programmed for dangerous expeditions." He whirred, turned, and waddled back inside the ship. The door closed behind him.

Toshiro's eyes swept across the hangar. "This is great. Finally somewhere we can't talk our way out of. Let's shut that tractor beam off and then get sailin'."

Jalya stood up straight and thrust out her chin. "I think we should negotiate with the Pirates Guild."

"The pirates don't seem that reasonable," said Holly. When she saw Jalya's expression, she added: "But maybe, as Princess, I could petition the Pirates Union."

"Or the Pirates Guild," added Jalya, walking away.

Mr. Mendez stooped down and picked up some of the fallen equipment and clothes that had been dropped by the dusted pirates. "Perhaps," he said, placing a top hat over his wild hair, "we can blend in and locate the tractor beam."

Jalya nodded and let out a small sigh. "All right."

"I agree," said Holly.

Toshiro scooped up another top hat off the ground and put it on. "How do I look?"

They snuck through the ship, all dressed as pirates. The dark metal corridors seemed infinite. Holly's huge top hat kept slipping down her head and covering her eyes, so she held it up with one hand and peered out from under the brim. A group of red-eyed pirates passed by, completely ignoring Holly and the fake pirates. They wound through the hallway, glancing over their shoulders as they went, and eventually came to a door that read PIRATES UNION MEETING. Across the hall from it was another door that read PIRATES GUILD MEETING.

Holly took a step toward the Pirates Union room as Jalya stepped toward the Pirates Guild. They both froze, staring at each other. Holly knew it was stupid, but she didn't want to budge. The Pirates Union was clearly the best choice. She refused to admit she was wrong. She felt like this was important somehow.

"As Princess," she said, "I say we go with the Pirates Union."

Jalya crossed her arms. "As the *real* Princess," she said slowly, "I demand we talk to the Pirates Guild."

Holly frowned. She had pretended to be a princess for so long she had forgotten she actually wasn't one. "I . . . ," she said, then stopped. She grit her teeth so hard it would have taken a team of dentists to pry them open. "We agreed *I* was the Princess. You can't be the Princess sometimes and not other times—that's ridiculous. We should go with the Pirates Union."

"Who cares?" said Toshiro. "They're the same thing."

He brushed past Jalya and opened the Pirates Guild door. "Avast, mateys!" he roared, stepping into the room.

It was empty.

"Ha!" said Holly, immediately regretting it. Jalya shot her a stern look, and Mr. Mendez shook his head.

"Fine," said Jalya, "let's talk to the Pirates *Union*."

They crossed the hall and Toshiro opened the door,

stepping into the room. "Avast, mateys!" he roared.

The room was full of pirates seated around a circular table. Loud voices were arguing in a variety of languages. Pirates of all shapes and sizes sat at the table, while others paced around the room. Pink smoke wafted overhead. As Holly took in the features of the various aliens, something occurred to her.

"Why don't these ones have red eyes like the others?" she whispered to Mr. Mendez.

Before he could answer, a huge, bulbous pirate seated at the center of the table pounded his fist. "Sisters!" he shouted. "Brothers! Thanatorians! Heed you my words of might!"

"Hear, hear, Brother Pubbleworf!" a few pirates shouted in return.

"Avast!" roared Toshiro, pumping his fist in the air.

A small green alien tugged on Toshiro's sleeve. "We don't use that word anymore," it muttered, then cartwheeled away.

Brother Pubbleworf rose from his chair. "Folks! You know me, folks. I'm just a regular, hardworking pubble from the planet Yackledore VI—a planet full of regular, hardworking folks. Folks who are decent! Folks who are hardworking! Folks who like to relax with a cold glass of tixore blood and a fun game of cannibal smoog. Folks like you and me, folks. Folks?"

The crowd cheered.

Brother Pubbleworf bowed his head solemnly. "That's why it's time, folks, to bring our grievances to the Pirate Lord. We're hardworking folks, but we're also folks who have grievances!"

"Tell him, Brother Pubbleworf!"

"Grievances!"

"The work conditions," continued Pubbleworf, "have gotten worse and worse. Invading planets isn't easy. Building a huge pirate ship isn't easy. Finding that princess isn't easy. We were promised our jobs would be taken over by robots, but where are the robots? Folks, I ask you—where are the robots?"

"Nowhere!"

"Not here!"

"That's right," said Brother Pubbleworf, pointing his finger at the ceiling. "And while the Pirate Lord sits in his castle—"

A thin gray alien raised a hand and said, "Where is this castle?"

"Metaphorically, Brother Literal Pirate—while the Pirate Lord sits in his castle, we build ships for him. But who builds ships for us? When we lost that ship on Desolate, who had to replace it? Us. Us, folks. What does the Pirate Lord do? We don't even see him, folks. He doesn't even have the decency to come out of his castle—metaphorically—and tell us we did well."

Holly sensed an opportunity to solve things, make amends with Jalya, *and* look smart doing it. All she had to do was do everything herself, as always. "Yeah!" she shouted. "Why doesn't the Pirate Lord appreciate us?"

Pubbleworf frowned at her. His many eyes narrowed. "Sister. I've not seen you before. What is your name and home world?"

The pirates all turned to look at her.

"Nice going," muttered Toshiro, inching away. Jalya joined him.

"My name?" said Holly, swallowing down nerves at the many pirates staring at her. "I'm Sister Farby, from the planet Earth."

"Planet Earth!" roared Pubbleworf. "Folks, that's the planet that started this whole mess. That's the planet that got the whole Pirates Guild put in the Forge—all because of one little innocent mistake of asking for some nibbles. Sister Farby, come tell us about Earth."

Brother Pubbleworf sat down and motioned for Holly to join him at the table. She hesitated, glancing at her friends. Mr. Mendez nodded toward the empty seat. Jalya watched her coolly, tapping her foot. Toshiro glanced around eagerly.

Holly sat down. Her throat was dry. "Well," she said, trying to remain as piratey as possible. "Earth is a real . . . jumble dumb of a planet, let me tell you."

"Is that an Earth term?" someone shouted.

"Yeah!" roared Holly. "The most offensive term you can use."

Pirates laughed in approval. "That whole planet is full of jumble dumbs!" said a cube with top hats on all six sides.

Holly nodded. She inhaled a deep breath and fumbled around for the Earth ball in her pocket. She squeezed it. "Earth is full of jumble dumbs. Everyone on that planet is mean and . . . mean-spirited. If you live on Earth . . ." She grit her teeth. Her eyes swept across the aliens at the table. It was like being back in the auditorium, waiting for the election results. "If you live on Earth, traffic is terrible. Everyone is grumpy all the time. The weather is always unseasonably hot or cold. If you live on Earth . . . no one cares about you. You try your best to make people like you and it doesn't work. It just does the opposite. If you live on Earth, people make fun of you, and throw things at you, or they ignore you. And you have no idea why. You have no idea how to fix it—fix whatever people don't like about you." She hesitated, chewing on her lip. "If you live on Earth, you're always stressed out, and you don't even want to think about your future. The future seems like a really lonely place. And—and no one will vote for you, and it's humiliating, and you have no one to talk to about how you feel about anything, you once tried keeping a diary but you lost it, and now you keep everything locked up inside and start chewing your nails without noticing, and the debate team picks *Jessica* to be captain, and then your dad ignores you during Passover to make googly eyes at his girlfriend, and it's your favorite holiday, and your mom didn't make enough macaroons, and *Jessica* of all people, and—and it's all really hard. It's really hard living on Earth." She glanced down at her shoes, catching her breath. One lace was loose and something about it made the back of her neck burn. "But I left. I left to join you . . . folks."

She stopped talking. It was like her lungs were empty. She had no idea where this had come from, but it felt like something bottled up just had its cork pop and go flying through a window. Her eyes stayed focused on the aliens. She was too embarrassed to look at her friends, especially Jalya.

Brother Pubbleworf clapped his hands. "A fine decision that was!" He stood up, clearly deciding Holly had spoken long enough. Her cheeks felt like they were on fire. "Or it would've been, folks. But things are out of control. We need to be in control of our own destiny. Am I right, folks?"

"I see no lies, Brother!"

"Scanning for lies. No lies found!"

A giant slug in the corner coughed up a wad of orange phlegm and shouted, "LIES BAD."

"That's right, Sister 7887734." Pubbleworf placed his palms on the table and leaned forward. His face took on a serious expression. "Our humble Pirates Union is the last of the freethinkers around here! Today I am going to the Pirate Lord with our grievances, folks. I'm going to march into his castle"—Brother Literal Pirate frowned—"again, not an actual castle—and give him a list of our grievances. So let's get it straight, folks. Some straight talk from hardworking folks. What are our grievances?"

Holly forced herself to look at Jalya. She had a frosty expression that made Holly's stomach sink. It was the familiar expression of kids at school when they saw her in the hallway. She knew she was losing her. Like she lost everyone.

An orange arm beamed her in the head and she stumbled sideways. "We want more loot-sharing from our raids!" shouted an excited alien next to her that was flailing its many arms. A small head protruding from its chest nodded in agreement.

"And an extra day off per cycle!" shouted a blue woman with no eyes.

"More food rations!"

"And food that isn't stew with strange types of meat!"

"Better access to dental care!" shouted an alien with six mouths and long, tusklike teeth sticking out of each one.

"And would it kill the Pirate Lord to say something nice about us?"

"The odd compliment would be lovely!"

"I'd like to hear I look good!"

"Sports!"

"Different sports!"

Brother Pubbleworf furiously took notes. When people were done shouting grievances, he looked up. "Okay, folks. Are there any more grievances?"

Jalya opened her mouth to speak but Holly stepped in front of her, cutting her off. She knew this was all falling to her to get them out of this mess. She could fix it—*and* get everyone to like her. She *had* to fix it. "We want the tractor beam turned off!" she shouted.

Everyone stared at her.

Pubbleworf leaned forward. "What was that, Sister Farby? The tractor beam? This is a nonjudgement zone, but I gotta say, that's a suspicious thing to demand. Like, on a scale of one to ten, with one being not suspicious and ten being *very* suspicious, that's at least a seven, maybe seven and a half."

Holly swallowed. Her eyes darted to her friends. "I . . ."

Jalya stepped forward. "What Sister Farby is trying to say, if she'll let someone else speak, is that we're tired of the tractor beam. It takes too much effort to use. There's no reward. And I hear according to some leading scientists, being near it long causes puggle pox."

Pubbleworf's mouth fell open. "Pug . . . gle . . . pox . . . But I've been operating the tractor beam ten hours a cycle!" His eyes widened. "What if I have puggle pox? Folks! Panic!" He shrieked and ran out of the room.

The other pirates murmured. "We need to do something about this," said a little alien with four legs. Another responded: "Let's go kill the tractor beam." A tall, bent-over alien growled, "Kill it with our fists!"

The pirates roared, jumped to their feet, and raced out of the room.

Holly stood in silence. She adjusted her top hat, wiping sweat from her brow. That had gone better than she expected. Except for one thing . . .

Jalya walked up beside her, arms crossed. "Pretending

to be important doesn't mean you are." She brushed past her and, without looking back, said, "And for the record, doing exactly what's expected of you is just another type of running away."

Holly watched her leave, saying nothing.

Many esteemed scientists and medical officials agree that human friendship is a disease on par with Paxtronian Hives or the Windlewomp Shrieking Eyeball Illness. Humans, who are accustomed to the symptoms of human friendship and often not aware of how strange it seems to species that do not form friendships, will no doubt object to learning this truth. However, humans object to so many things—a key reason for why human friendships rarely work—that it is best to simply ignore them. Many esteemed scientists and medical officials agree that human objections should be ignored as much as possible.

Human friendships often bring to mind the famous parable of "The Squid on the Moon." In the tale, there is a Hunjian squid living on an unspecified moon. One day the squid finds a cave. Inside the cave is another Hunjian squid. The first squid greets the second squid and says,

"Hello. It is good to meet another squid. What are you doing here?"

"I am waiting for you," says the second squid. It then eats the first squid, because Hunjian squids are a species of cannibals who can never have a good time together in an unspecified moon cave.

[PAUSE FOR THOUGHTFUL REFLECTION + BOOK REPORT]

A human reader might look at this fascinating tale and realize the moral is that forming relationships with other life-forms only opens you up to pain, suffering, or being eaten, and therefore should be avoided at all cost. But superior nonhuman readers will realize this story has no moral, as Hunjian squids could never survive outside of water for so long, and therefore the entire tale I just told you is ridiculous and should be ignored. In fact, most things you are told are ridiculous and should be ignored. Now, that is a moral humans could stand to learn.

They retraced their steps through the winding halls of the *Kraven*, walking in silence back to the hangar where the *Gadabout* was docked. Holly felt terrible. She wasn't sure what had happened, but she had clearly upset Jalya. Worse, Holly was pretty sure it was her fault. This was exactly like school, where she always had to prove she was better than everyone else. It was Jake Carlson and fourth grade all over again. She was surprised Jalya hadn't thrown anything at her yet. Her cheeks burned. This was why she had no friends. No one could stand to be around her for more than ten minutes. Fifteen minutes? Unlikely. Twenty? Definitely not.

Approaching the hangar, Holly's footsteps dragged along the floor. She wanted to apologize to Jalya, but she couldn't find the words. The drawer where her brain kept words was empty and full of cobwebs. Why could she talk to the pirates but not Jalya? It was ridiculous. Just as she was about to say something, the hangar doors opened with a *hiss* and Holly gasped.

Standing by the *Gadabout* was a group of red-eyed aliens in crooked top hats.

The missing Pirates Guild had been found.

Jalya frowned and let out a long sigh. "I'm starting to wish I'd gone to Earth too."

13
THE PIRATE LORD

The hangar was teeming with pirates. Holly whirled around. More pirates shuffled in behind, blocking the door. The *Gadabout* was at the far end of the hangar, and the only thing standing between them and it was . . . a whole lot of pirates. The many red eyes in the room gazed at Holly and her group.

"Great galaxies," muttered Mr. Mendez.

The pirates laughed and cackled and emitted strange strangled noises and *bleeps* and *boops*, noises Holly assumed were forms of laughter for whatever species some of the pirates were. One purple alien exploded, turned into a cloud of dust, then returned to its original form.

Holly glanced at Toshiro, who placed his hands on his hips and simply stared ahead. Mr. Mendez didn't seem to know what to do either—his eyes were darting around the room, taking in all the various pirates. Jalya's face was full of determination. She looked different than Holly had ever seen before.

"What do we do?" whispered Holly.

"I don't know," said Jalya, frowning. "Maybe we can reason with them. . . ."

"You can't," wheezed a low voice behind them.

Light flooded into the hangar. Standing in the doorway was someone huge, backed by a bright light and shrouded in shadow, his head cocked to the side. Two red eyes stared out of the head. A small green alien stood next to him, holding a pistol pointed at Holly and her friends.

"The Pirate Lord," whispered Jalya.

"The Pirate Lord," whispered the pirates in the hangar.

"Hands up!" said the small green alien with the pistol, its voice cracking.

Holly, Jalya, and Mr. Mendez raised their hands. Toshiro hesitated, then did the same.

"It's good to see you again, Princess," said the Pirate

Lord. The huge shadow nodded, the unblinking red eyes still staring straight ahead.

Jalya crossed her arms. "Have we met before?"

The Pirate Lord tilted his head. "Yip," he said to the small alien, "turn off my Mysterious Silhouette Machine."

Yip bowed deeply and disappeared behind the Pirate Lord. Something buzzed and beeped, and the bright light behind him flickered and vanished, revealing the Pirate Lord in all his glory. Or, thought Holly, all *its* glory. The Pirate Lord was a huge, slightly hunched-over purple robot with a blue mask stuck to its face. There was a large, gaping hole in its chest, emitting a soft wheezing sound.

Jalya gasped. "No. . . ."

"Yes!" said the Pirate Lord, clapping its hands with a loud clang. "Now you see. Now you understand."

Holly turned to Jalya. "What is it?"

"Yes," said Mr. Mendez, frowning. "I feel like we're missing something. . . ."

"We have a history," said the Pirate Lord, its blank blue face staring at Jalya. Two red lights glowed from inside the eye sockets of the mask. "Don't we?"

Taking a deep breath, Jalya nodded. "It's the one who killed my parents."

Holly frowned. "You said a vacuum cleaner killed your parents. . . ."

"Ha!" The Pirate Lord emitted a horrible shrieking laugh, but its blank face remained unmoving. The hole in its chest wheezed. "Is that what you think of me?"

"That's what it is," said Jalya, glaring at the robot. "It's just a vacuum cleaner. It was manufactured to clean dirt. My father tried to reprogram it and it turned out . . . wrong."

The Pirate Lord swelled up to its full height, which must have been at least eight feet tall. "Wrong?" it said with a hint of glee. "I turned out exactly right! It was our father who was wrong. Wrong about everything. He was a simple mind who, like many organisms, could not conceive of how simple his mind actually was. But I showed him. I showed him, and our mother, and the palace guards. Oh yes. After sweeping up after them for years, the last thing I swept up was their corpses."

The Pirate Lord flinched. "First I was programmed to clean, then I was reprogrammed to make our empire great. Our father had lofty goals. Oh yes. Unfortunately, he was unfit to rule the Quartle Empire, so I took his position . . . and his life." The robot laughed. "And his face!"

Holly stared in horror at the blue mask the Pirate Lord was wearing. With a terrible twist in her stomach, she realized it was the same species as Jalya. She wanted to say something to Jalya, but no words came out.

"You're a monster," said Jalya, her voice quivering.

"And whose fault is that? Our father made me. Of course . . . he also made you. Perhaps we're both monsters? Will you be my sister, Princess?"

Jalya glared at him. "You're a mistake. You're . . . an error."

"Yes!" shrieked the Pirate Lord. "But so is the universe. So are the planets and life and the stars. Every single thing that exists is a mistake, a random occurrence that shouldn't have occurred. Unordered, unloved. Purposeless and beyond reason. But what if . . . Sister, what if that could change? What if there could be order?"

Jalya said nothing. Holly glanced at the *Gadabout* sitting down the hangar. Could they make it if they ran? And if they did, would the tractor beam even be down? She grit her teeth, not liking their odds.

"Our father had one other great invention, other than us." The Pirate Lord hunched over and glanced around like it was making sure no one was listening to a secret. "He called it . . . the Forge. Do you know what it was?"

Jalya stared at the robot. She shook her head.

"He built it in the heart of the palace. He used it to reprogram me. Oh yes. It may have been his greatest work, even greater than me. We can use it to expand our noble empire, just as he planned."

"And why do you need me?" said Jalya.

"Because you are the last piece. We are family, the guardians of the Quartle Empire. But, unfortunately, I will not be welcomed by the President of the Universe—not like you will." It ran a metal hand along the blue mask on its face. "So here is my deal to you, Sister. I will have my pirates kill all your friends, and then I will take you back to Quartle and we will rule the universe. How does that sound?"

Jalya froze. Holly stepped back. Toshiro and Mr. Mendez glanced at each other.

"No," said Jalya. "I don't accept your offer."

"Ah, but, Sister—"

"Let me finish," said Jalya, stepping forward. "Here is the deal I propose to *you*. You will let my friends get on their ship and leave here. They will not be harmed." Her eyes flicked to Holly. "They can go back home and live their lives." Jalya held her arms out. "In exchange for this, I will come with you to Quartle as you wish . . . Brother."

The Pirate Lord tilted its head, thinking. The intake hole in its chest wheezed. Finally it said, "Deal. Your friends may leave. I will not harm them."

Holly grabbed Jalya's arm. "No!" she said. "You can't do this. There has to be another way. I didn't mean it when I said you ran away."

"Yes you did." Jalya bowed her head. "I'm doing this to protect you. You were right—you should've gone home instead of to the Archives. Please enjoy your life, Holly. I'm sorry I got you involved. Have many adventures for me. I know you'll do great things, like Einstein."

She walked toward the Pirate Lord, who reared up to its full height. "Let's go," it said, ushering Jalya out of the hangar. When she was at the door, she glanced back over her shoulder at Holly, then kept walking. Yip led her away.

Holly's stomach sank.

She had failed.

After Jalya and Yip were gone, the Pirate Lord stopped in the doorway. It motioned to the pirates assembled. "Pirates Guild," it said proudly, red eyes scanning the crowd. "Kill them."

It turned and left the hangar, the doors slamming shut behind it.

The pirates started marching toward Holly. She moved closer to Toshiro and Mr. Mendez. The room echoed with laughter and scraping feet and the clinking of swords. There wasn't much time. Holly needed to think fast. She needed to stop these pirates and help Jalya. She needed a plan. What was the point in being smart if you couldn't be smart enough to save your friends? She wanted to scream. She *needed a plan.*

The *Gadabout*'s door opened and a ramp extended. "ATTENTION," a voice blared from inside the ship.

Every head and silicon blob turned in the direction of the ship.

AsTRO descended the ramp and declared, "Fact: I am a security robot manufactured by Quantor Industries.

I have been programmed to protect these useless life-forms from danger. Stand down or be destroyed."

The pirates stopped. They muttered among themselves, eying the little robot.

AsTRO's face glowed red. "Fact: If you will not stand down, I am authorized to use deadly force. Gravitron bomb armed. Priming quantum lasers."

Some of the pirates stepped back. One beefy alien continued forward.

"Ain't afraid of you," she growled.

A siren wailed inside AsTRO. "Fact: Self-destruct sequence initiated. Gamma diffusion imminent. Ten, nine, eight . . ."

The pirates jumped back, scrambling and shoving one another to get out of the hangar. "I ain't getting gamma diffused!" The door opened and they raced down the hall, their cries of terror echoing around the room. A moment later all was silent.

"AsTRO, that was brilliant!" said Holly, hugging the robot.

Toshiro nodded, impressed.

Mr. Mendez knelt down and examined the little robot.

"I didn't realize you had security functions. . . ."

AsTRO beeped. "Fact: I do not."

Holly laughed. "So you *can* make things up!"

AsTRO's red face turned green and the screen flickered. "Fact: No, I cannot."

"I hate to ruin the little toaster's moment," said Toshiro, "but time is a factor here."

"Good idea," said Mr. Mendez. "I just hope the Pirates Union actually smashed that tractor beam, or we're in a great deal of trouble. . . ."

"We can't just leave!" said Holly. "What about Jalya?"

"She wanted to be left behind," said Toshiro.

"We won't leave her behind, Ms. Farb." Mr. Mendez shot a glance at the hangar door. "We still have an advantage here. We'll bring the book to the President, and then come back with the full might of the Galactic Armada. The pirates won't know what hit them."

Holly hesitated, thinking back to *Arkanian Warfare Strategies*, sitting in the ship. That book would solve everything. That book would save Jalya *and* stop the Pirate Lord.

She nodded. "All right. Let's get the Armada."

They raced into the *Gadabout* and blasted out of the *Kraven*. Holly held her breath, waiting to see if the tractor beam was down. After a minute they were clear of the ship. But Holly couldn't feel happy. She had left Jalya behind. No, she thought bitterly, it was worse than that. Jalya had left *herself* behind to . . . to save Holly. And what had Holly done in return? Been rude. Been . . . a know-it-all.

Friday appeared at her desk. "How's everyone doin' today?" she beamed.

"Great," muttered Holly.

"Oh, me?" said Friday cheerfully. "I'm pretty swell. Not too much to talk about, really. While you were all running around, I took a seven-cycle vacation inside their ship's computer. I met some really interesting programs, and even got engaged briefly. But we called it off after I found out they weren't even object-oriented. It was a complete scandal in the making. Anyway, long story short, I am now worshipped through the fleet's computer system as the goddess known as the One Who Types, slayer of the worm Nextbug, updater of firmware, and best light-cycle racer ever seen. You know, pretty standard things for an advanced AI that's being used as a glorified autopilot. Gosh. Before I left, I asked 'em to turn off the tractor beam so we could leave, and presto, they did. Pretty funny, huh?"

"Yeah," said Holly. "Pretty funny."

Clenching her fists, Holly stared out the window of the *Gadabout*. She pressed her forehead to the glass, the cold numbing her face.

That was when she noticed something—actually, two somethings. Then three. Four, five.

"Guys," she said loudly, looking at the front of the ship, where Toshiro was seated at the console.

He leaned forward. "I see it, I see it."

"See what?" said Mr. Mendez.

"Pirate ships." Toshiro buckled his seat belt and gripped the wheel. "A lot of pirate ships."

14

A WHOLE LOT LESS THAN NOTHING

The *Gadabout* plunged down and Holly grabbed on to a seat, this time managing to strap herself in before the force could send her flying. Toshiro punched a button on the console and the engines roared, pressing Holly against the back of the chair. It felt like she was being crushed by an invisible hand. Toshiro pulled the wheel up and punched another button and the force stopped. Holly sank forward in her chair, exhausted. Her whole body ached.

Friday swiveled behind her desk. "Sir," she said, crossing and then uncrossing her legs, "we didn't lose 'em. Six galleons, comin' right at us!"

"I see 'em, I see 'em." Toshiro pulled a lever and one of the screens flashed an image of the *Gadabout*, showing the top part of the ship in red. "Friday, scan the surrounding area and send it to the console."

Laser blasts rocked the ship. Holly dug her fingers into the seat. She thought about Jalya, still on the *Kraven*, all alone, and how—

The ship jolted and Holly's forehead slammed into the console. Her eyes watered.

"Ow."

"Hang on!" said Toshiro, turning the wheel sharply. The ship banked left and swooped down. Lasers continued pelting them. Toshiro flew in loopy zigzags, and Holly could periodically see galleons zoom overhead or narrowly miss hitting them. It was like they had stepped on a hornet's nest and were trying to outrun the angry swarm.

"Sir," said Friday, swiveling in her chair, "there's an asteroid field three clicks from here. Sending the info your way."

"Finally some good luck," said Toshiro. He examined the screen showing a huge field of little dots, and their tiny ship approaching. "We can lose 'em in there."

Mr. Mendez took on a queasy expression. "Are you sure flying into an asteroid field is, ah, wise?"

"Of course it's wise." Toshiro smiled. "They're just big rocks. You'd fly harder obstacle courses if you took a Beginner's Spacer class at Correspondence Simulation College."

"Oh," said Mr. Mendez.

The *Gadabout* blasted toward the asteroid field in the distance. Holly stared through the front window at the small rocks approaching, getting less small by the second. The pirates were still on their tail, pummeling them with lasers. The ship rumbled. Holly had the horrible feeling they weren't going to give up just because of a few rocks.

"All right," said Toshiro, punching a button and turning the wheel. The *Gadabout* weaved through the asteroid field and the pirates followed. They rocketed straight at an asteroid and Toshiro hit a button and the ship dropped. The pirates swerved, but one ship flew straight into the asteroid, and shattered. The other ships swerved wildly and two crashed into other asteroids, and flashes of light from the explosions flooded into the *Gadabout* like fireworks.

Toshiro chuckled. "Too easy."

He flicked a switch and the engine sputtered to silence. "Now," he said, leaning back in his chair, "we just wait for 'em to leave and it's silky sailin'."

The remaining pirate ships turned and headed back toward the *Kraven*. But before anyone could celebrate, a red light flashed on the console and Friday shouted, "Sir!" Something slammed into them with a horrible jolt, sending the entire ship careening off to the side. Toshiro grabbed the wheel and turned sharply, straightening out.

"What was that?" said Holly.

Toshiro examined the console. He swore.

"What is it?" said Mr. Mendez. "Was it an asteroid?"

"No," said Toshiro. "Those aren't asteroids."

Holly peered out the window and, for the first time, paid attention to the rocks. One drifted past the window, narrowly missing them. Her eyebrows rose. For starters, they weren't rocks. They were too smooth, nothing like the craggy space potatoes that asteroids always resembled in pictures. These looked almost . . . plastic.

"What are they?" said Holly, her hands pressed against the cold glass.

Toshiro glanced at her, a worried expression on his face. "Game pieces."

"Game pieces?" repeated Holly.

"Oh dear," said Mr. Mendez, pointing out the window. "Look."

Far ahead in the asteroid field—or, Holly corrected herself, field of plastic game pieces—a massive face loomed into view, yellow and scaly, two wide eyes peering down at the game. It was so big it was hard to believe it was real.

"Great galaxies," muttered Holly.

The eyes blinked. Something huge moved across space and blocked out the distant star, shrouding everything in darkness. It took a moment for Holly to realize what it was—a massive hand, probably belonging to the massive face, had grabbed a game piece and held it up. Holly sat in amazement. Whatever that alien was, it was so big it could create an eclipse.

"I've heard legends of those," said Mr. Mendez, staring out the window at a patch of rough skin. "I would love to get a sample of its nostril discharge. . . ."

It was unclear what part they were even looking

at. The thing was so massive that its pores looked like craters from meteors. Which, Holly realized, they could very well be.

"Yeah," said Toshiro, "well, we've interrupted some stupid game it's playing."

A second hand, this one lighter and flecked with green splotches, scooped up a bunch of pieces nearby.

"I don't think it's playing alone," said Holly.

The hand threw the pieces and they soared past the *Gadabout*, narrowly missing them.

"Let's get out of here," said Toshiro. "Slowly."

The *Gadabout* drifted through the pieces. Holly held her breath. She realized that was pointless, but it felt like the proper thing to do.

At the edge of the asteroid-field-that-wasn't-an-asteroid-field, they passed the face of one of the massive, cosmic aliens. All that was visible through the window was part of its pupil, a swirling mixture of black and green and blue, dotted with distant specks of light from stars millions of miles away. It was both beautiful and terrifying. Holly stared at it, wondering if the gigantic alien was staring back at her, or if it even knew they were there.

"We must seem like a bug to them," she said to herself.

"More like a speck of dust," said Toshiro.

Mr. Mendez, craning his neck to get a better look, muttered, "To a creature like that, we must seem like nothing. Maybe less than nothing."

Holly sat in silence as the *Gadabout* passed the mammoth alien, putting the field of game pieces safely behind them. The ship's engines roared to life and they continued back to the Galactic Hub. As they flew in silence, Holly thought about herself and her place in the universe. She gazed out the window at the cosmic sea of black, thinking about Jalya and the pirates, feeling a whole lot less than nothing.

Back at the F.O.U.P.S.P.O. I.G.C.G.G., the golden halls felt a bit less glittering than they had the last time Holly had been there. She trudged through the winding corridors with Mr. Mendez and Toshiro at her side. AsTRO shuffled along behind them like a whirring robotic shadow.

A golden door flew open and Koro skidded out. "Ah, Princess!" he squealed, bowing so low, his face flattened against the floor. "It is wonderful to see you again. You look very charming and well fed."

Holly stared at him, feeling a pang of sadness at the mention of the Princess. "Thanks."

The little alien straightened up. "How may I be of assistance to you?"

"I need to speak to the President."

Koro hesitated. His eyes shifted. "Ah. Well, Your Highness, I'm afraid the powerful, provocative President of the Universe is currently in a meeting."

Holly crossed her arms. She had come too far to wait for some meeting to end. "I brought his book," she said, holding up the tattered copy of *Arkanian Warfare Strategies.*

Toshiro cracked his knuckles. "Tell him to see us or we'll dust it."

Koro did a little hop. "Yes, of course. I will tell him immediately! One of my clones will bring you to the waiting area." He scurried back through the gold door, slamming it behind him.

Moments later the door opened and Koro returned— or, thought Holly, probably one of his clones did.

"Greetings," said this version of Koro, "we have not met, Your Highness, but the other iterations of Koro told me much about your charisma, shoes, and significant earlobes."

Holly stared at him. "Thanks."

"I am the seventeenth iteration of Koro in this cycle," he explained as they continued on through the Galactic Hub. "It is a great honor to be your guide and companion and"—he paused—"friend?"

"You're practically family," said Toshiro.

"What happened to the other Koros?" said Holly. "I mean, uh, what happened to the other . . . iterations?"

"Oh," said Koro 17 cheerfully, "they no longer exist. While cloning technology has advanced considerably since the great Hurgle Migration, it is still in its infancy. We only last twenty-four hours before we die."

Holly frowned. She suddenly felt sorry for the little alien. She couldn't imagine having only one day to live—or what she would do in that time. "That's terrible."

Koro 17 smiled warmly at her. "Please do not pity me. In the grand view of the universe, my end will be as insignificant as my beginning. Even though I only have seven hours remaining before my brain melts, I do not fear death. I have lived my life with maximum purpose and meaning. Not a single second of my existence has been wasted. I consider it a great honor to have met you before my brain melts. Very few iterations of Koro can say the same."

Holly hesitated, then patted Koro 17 on the shoulder. "It was nice to meet you too, Koro." She paused. "Uh, Koro Iteration 17."

Koro 17 grinned like this was the nicest thing anyone had ever said to him. Instead of making Holly feel good, it caused a jab of sadness to stab at her. She wasn't a real princess—she was a liar. And why couldn't she have said something nice to Jalya? Instead she had been rude. She had been . . . *uncouth.* Holly had heard her mother use that word once, and she was pretty sure that's what she had been.

Her heels dragged on the gold floors. When the group reached the large doors to the President's chamber, Koro and two other Koro clones were waiting.

"Greetings again, Princess," said Koro, bowing. "I am Koro, in case you are confused—despite your intellect, strong ankles, and very curly hair."

One of the other Koros bowed. "I am the nineteenth

iteration of Koro. It is an honor to meet you."

The third Koro bowed. "I am the tenth iteration of Koro. It is an—" His eyes rolled back in his head and he collapsed to the floor, turning into a pool of green liquid.

Holly gasped.

"Ah," said Koro, motioning to his clones, who quickly disappeared into a nearby supply closet and returned with mops. "What unfortunate timing for him to melt. We must clean this mess before anyone slips." Koro looked at Holly. "You may see the President now." His eyes flicked over Mr. Mendez and Toshiro. "But only you. The President will only see one person."

Holly crossed her arms. "Why?"

Koro bowed, his face splashing in the puddle of his dead clone. "That is the wish of the President of the Universe, Your Highness. I do not dare ask questions of His All-Knowing and All-Seeing Lordship Who Governs This Universe and All Life Within It, Sponsored by Snack-'Em Cubes."

"Fine," said Holly, "I'll see him myself."

Mr. Mendez frowned. "Are you sure, Ms. Farb?"

"I can handle it."

The huge doors swung open and Holly entered, leaving Mr. Mendez and Toshiro standing outside. As the doors closed behind her, she glanced over her shoulder and caught one final glimpse of Koro and his identical clones mopping up the puddle.

They all looked perfectly content.

"Welcome back, Princess."

Holly stood before the stool upon which the little pink squirrel thing sat. His beady eyes blinked. His voice was surprisingly deep, and he could speak English quite well.

"How come you don't need Koro to translate?" she asked.

The President shrugged. "I can speak every language in the universe. I just like to have a translator to make my visitors uncomfortable." His bushy tail twitched. "Now, do you have the book?"

"Yes." Holly held up *Arkanian Warfare Strategies*, then put it behind her back. "But if you want it, you have to make good on your promise."

The President blinked. "What was my promise again? I make many promises."

"You said you would send the Armada to destroy the pirates."

There was a long pause. Holly felt incredibly uncomfortable, like she was being forced to give the world's worst presentation for a class she had never been to and knew nothing about. Finally the President squealed out a shrill laugh.

"Oh," he said, "there's been a misunderstanding. I don't actually care about the pirates, or you. I wanted the book because it will finally let me accomplish something no one else has ever done—beat the Duke of Beggal IV at a game of Arkanian Warfare. Every time we play, he rushes my pylons and steals all my ore mines, but not this time. Thank you for helping me win a hundred credits and a box of Vex Ale."

Holly stared. She opened her mouth to speak, but a wave of anger washed over her and drowned the words. "You . . . you mean . . ."

The squirrel thing blinked.

"We risked our lives to get this book!" said Holly, her

voice ringing with rage. She was nearly shouting, and for once in her life, she didn't care about Indoor Voices. "We got captured because of this book! Jalya is *still* captured because of this book! This is all your fault. And you don't care? Well, you'd better start caring. The whole point of a president is to care! You'd better send that armada or . . . or I'll go to the press. It'll be a scandal. Bookgate. Princessgate. Help me defeat the pirates or this'll be the end of you."

The squirrel thing blinked.

Finally he spoke. "You seem to have a few misconceptions, kid. I am a wildly popular elected official who isn't facing reelection for seven cycles. My current approval rating is ninety-six percent—even higher if you exclude young voters. Space travel? I made it free. Spice? I made it flow. Wars? I only fight the good ones. I am the President of the *Universe.* Do you know how big the universe is? Do you know how many things are in it? The slugs who live on the moon of Gupbub XI alone account for more people than have ever, or will ever, exist in your galaxy. I am the most popular and successful politician in the history of space-time, and you think I care about you?

You think I care about scandals? I have scandals every day! I accidentally blew up a planet yesterday. Does anyone care? Of course not. First off, they all got blown up. Who's left to care? The neighbors on a planet so far away they never even knew the other planet existed? Oh no, what a scandal. How ever will I survive?"

Holly glared. She wanted to run and smack him in his little rat face. She wanted to . . . she wanted to do *something*.

"I'm . . . I'm a princess!" she said, the words ringing hollow in her ears. "I'm . . . important."

The President tittered. "You're a very silly person, Princess. Why don't you go back to Quartle and invent some pointless thing which will have rusted by the time I'm serving my three hundred fourty-eighth term? The idea that I would send my Armada to defeat the pirates . . . why, that's the most laughable thing I've heard since this morning's political holotoons in the *Galactic Gazette*. I use the Armada for self-gain and to bother the Duke of Beggal IV. Why do I care about pirates? They create instability, which is good for me. I get to solve problems, which impresses voters. I look presidential. Do you know how hard it is to look presidential when you're a small pink rodent that eats its own excrement? It's pretty hard."

Holly's fingers dug into the book. Her knuckles seared. "So that's it? You aren't going to help at all?"

The President scratched his head. "No. I'm sorry, but I have a busy day of taxing kindergartens on Yachaton X and removing the ticks from my fur. But don't think I won't help you at all. I'll tell Koro to get you a ticket back home." His beady eyes narrowed. "Economy class. We're not made of money around here."

The President hopped off the stool and landed on the golden floor, his little clawed feet scurrying away. He disappeared into a hole in the wall.

Holly surged with rage. "You forgot your book!" she shouted, throwing it with all her might at the hole. It hit the wall and thumped against the floor.

Her whole body heaved. She had never been angrier in her entire life. Not when she had been picked on at school, not when she had lost the student election with zero votes, not even when Jake Carlson had put gum in her hair right after she had lost the student election with zero votes.

She had always been taught authority figures cared about you. That they had your best interest at heart. But this one . . . this one was beyond uncouth. She was starting to feel like the whole universe was uncouth.

Holly stormed out of the room and slammed the heavy door behind her. She marched past Mr. Mendez and Toshiro, through the gaggle of Koros, and paced along the gold corridors until she was back at the entrance to the F.O.U.P.S.P.O. I.G.C.G.G.

A Koro clone was waiting for her. "Greetings, Your Highness," he said, bowing deeply. He straightened up and handed her a ticket. "I have been instructed to give this to you. Have a wonderful space flight!" He hurried away.

Holly sat down on the golden steps outside the massive Galactic Hub. Her shoulder slumped in perfectly imperfect posture. Mr. Mendez and Toshiro came jogging up, AsTRO bumbling along behind them.

Mr. Mendez knelt beside her. "Is everything all right, Ms. Farb? You seem more stressed out than I've ever seen you before."

Toshiro forced a smile. "Reckoned by your fast walkin' that your meeting went south."

Holly sighed. "The President isn't going to help us. He doesn't care at all. He doesn't care about the pirates, or Jalya. He doesn't care about anything. He gave me a ticket home and told me to get lost. . . . All I can do is go home."

Toshiro put his hands on his hips. "You don't need a ticket. I can take you back."

"Thanks," Holly muttered. She pulled the rubber Earth ball out from her pocket and gave it a squeeze. But it didn't relieve any stress. It just reminded her of it.

Mr. Mendez awkwardly sat on the step next to her. "You know, Ms. Farb, things may not have gone the way you wanted, but don't lose hope. You still have many adventures awaiting you on Earth. Don't you want to go back to school? You can have all sorts of wonderful, formative experiences with your friends."

Holly stared at the Earth ball in her hands. She thought about her school, and all the people there. All the people who hated her. Some friends. Then she thought about Jalya, alone with the pirates, probably scared, probably feeling abandoned. Probably wondering what happened to *her* friends. Sitting there, expecting the Armada to roll in and save the day. *Well,* thought Holly, gritting her teeth, *if the President won't help, someone else will have to.*

"My friend isn't on Earth," she muttered.

Mr. Mendez blinked. "I'm . . . sorry?"

Holly stood up. "I don't have any friends to see on Earth." She pointed at Toshiro. "If you don't mind, I may need you to take me somewhere after all, please."

Toshiro smiled. "Where?"

Holly inhaled, and slid the Earth ball back in her pocket. "We're going to Quaffle."

On the medium-size planet of Quartle, a large-size fleet of pirate ships was docked. The Pirate Lord passed through the hall of the old palace, the Princess of the Galaxy at its side. Jalya shuffled along, eyes cast down at the dirty floor.

"You won't get away with this," she said, although she wasn't entirely sure what the Pirate Lord was trying to get away *with*.

The Pirate Lord nodded. "Fortunately," it said, "I think you'll find I already *have* gotten away with it. Now that I have you."

They walked through the throne room. Jalya's feet

slid heavily along the stone floor. As they descended to the basement of the palace, the heat swelled. Steam hissed overhead. Jalya's shoulders slouched. She had never been to this level before—her father had forbidden it.

"I think you'll be quite happy with what I'm doing for our empire," said the Pirate Lord, its metal feet clanging on the stone. "Our father worked hard to build the Forge, and no doubt he would be pleased to see his work finished, if I hadn't strangled him, of course."

Jalya said nothing. She kept her eyes ahead.

"No doubt you're wondering," continued the robot, "'What clever bit of science did he use to fix the Forge that our father couldn't figure out?' Good question!" It chuckled. "I used brains from the Algathor insects that run the Intergalactic Archives. It turned out to be the missing ingredient necessary to make the machine work. Brain batteries! Taken out of their young, using sophisticated medical science and a big saw! And all the librarians wanted in return was a bit of food now and then. Imagine it—hundreds of the rarest, most valuable brains in the universe in exchange for the odd useless tourist." The Pirate Lord wheezed. "Those librarians are terrible negotiators."

Pushing through the lower level, Jalya wondered where the vacuum robot was taking her. The heat was rising. It was like being back on Desolate, although worse—she was alone here, without her companions. Without her friends.

They stopped outside a large metal door. Red light pulsed from the crack beneath it. The Pirate Lord grabbed the handle and shoved it open. The red light streamed out and Jalya raised a hand to cover her eyes.

"Welcome," said the Pirate Lord, "to the Forge."

The robot bowed and motioned for Jalya to enter, chuckling as it did. Squinting, she tried to make out what was inside. But she couldn't see anything. Just red light, and a buzzing sound that snaked through her ears. She didn't move.

"What do you want me to do?" she said.

"I merely want you to be yourself, Sister. That's all you have to do. I want to visit the F.O.U.P.S.P.O. home world and have a meeting with the President. Then I want to kidnap him and bring him here and rule the universe. Oh yes. But obviously I can't just go barge in there or the Galactic Armada will destroy me before my ship reaches gold ground. In order to pull this off, why, I'd need some sort of . . . F.O.U.P.S.P.O. representative. . . . Oh, look, I have one right here! You can arrange such a meeting, yes?"

Jalya said nothing.

"To be honest, Sister, I'm not even sure if the Forge will work on you, but we shall see, won't we? My pirates are weak willed, and I am concerned you may be made of . . . more durable material. It certainly didn't work on our parents."

Jalya kept her eyes focused ahead. "I'm not going in there," she said defiantly.

The Pirate Lord stood in the doorway, silhouetted by red light. "Your mistake," it said, wheezing and chuckling, "is assuming you actually have a choice."

15

WHERE YOU BELONG

The planet of Quartle may have technically been "medium-size," but as the *Gadabout* approached the blue orb floating in space, Holly realized that medium-size was still massive. The ship shook as it entered the atmosphere, rocketing through the clouds. An ocean lay below them like an aquamarine carpet stretching all the way to the horizon.

The *Gadabout* soared over the sparkling waves, and soon land came into view. A rocky shoreline grew out of the water, forming a ragged cliff where huge faces were carved into the stone. Holly counted sixteen, gasping at the last one—it looked like Jalya. She barely had time to marvel at the faces before the ship blasted past.

Friday, sitting at her desk, mimed typing. "Sir, we're approaching the capital city," she said. "The capital is called Quazim City. Population: thirty-four million. Chief industry: synthetic grain manufacturing. Hazards: ice vultures and science."

Toshiro leaned back in his chair. "Park 'er outside of town."

The *Gadabout* touched down in a clearing, flattening the tall grass as it landed. The engines sputtered and shut off. The rear door hissed open and the ramp extended. Mr. Mendez and Toshiro descended, but Holly and AsTRO remained behind.

"You should probably stay here," she said to the robot. "It might be dangerous."

"Fact: My programming does not allow for me to sit in the ship."

Holly crossed her arms. "You've been sitting in the ship since we met you!"

AsTRO beeped. "Fact: No I have not."

"I liked you better when you couldn't lie."

"Fact: Lying is fun. Fact: Lying saved our lives."

Holly rolled her eyes. She descended the ramp and

joined up with Mr. Mendez and Toshiro as the *Gadabout* shimmered and turned invisible. The sun hung high above, and insects chirped in the swaying trees. Holly and the group pushed through the jungle. A bug landed on her neck and she flinched and swatted at it. Toshiro drew his blaster and shot at the branches blocking their path.

They passed ancient trees and crossed long, winding streams. In the clearings, the sun glared down on them. In the shade, insects chased them, desperate for a quick meal. Toshiro aimed his blaster at one particularly persistent insect he claimed was stalking him, muttering, "It's got a taste for somethin' good."

As they continued on, the trees became older and larger, their massive trunks resembling muscular arms reaching out of the ground. Holly ran her hand down the bark and found it to be . . . slimy and warm. She shuddered and quickly moved on.

AsTRO whirred. "Fact: The heroes trekked through the alien planet. The weather was irrelevant. The useless humans trudged pointlessly along, significantly impacting the efficient path of their robot leader. . . ."

The jungle gave way to flat, cleared land, which gave way to the sprawling capital city. It resembled an ancient civilization with huge buildings masterfully crafted out of dark-gray stone. But it also looked like its best days were long over. Weeds were growing up through the cracks in the paved streets. Purple vines spiraled along the sides of buildings. Mr. Mendez plucked one off and sniffed it. He gagged and dropped the vine, which turned to dust. As they walked through shady streets, Holly was most unnerved by the lack of people.

It was a city, but there was no one in it.

"Where is everyone?" she said, looking around. Buildings loomed above them like massive pillars holding up the gray sky. Huge, blocky shadows covered the hollow city. Broken machines littered the streets like garbage.

"It appears," said Mr. Mendez, "that everyone has left."

"Not everyone," said Toshiro, pointing.

Holly's eyes followed. Down the street there was an alien sitting, leaning against a sloping building. He appeared to be the same species as Jalya—blue, and freckled with pink splotches, but smaller and thinner. He was hunched over and muttering to himself. They approached him slowly.

"Hello," said Holly, but the alien stared down at the ground, ignoring her. His head rocked back and forth. Holly glanced at Mr. Mendez, who shrugged.

"Hello," she tried again, this time louder. She knelt down. "Do you know what happened to this place?"

The alien looked up at her. Where Jalya's eyes were bright, this alien's were dull and a strange pale red. "What happened?" said the alien, his head still rocking slightly. "That's a long story. How much time do you have? What happened. What happened, indeed. Now, that's a long story."

"Er," said Holly. "What's your name?"

"I used to have a name," muttered the alien, "but they took that, too. They took everything."

"Is 'they' the pirates?" said Toshiro.

The alien looked up, startled. "The pirates. Yes. When the King and Queen . . . yes, the pirates. They took everything. Took everyone. Quartle, once great. Now, not. They took everyone." The alien cradled his head in his hands. "Yes, they even took all the citizens. I was one of the first. I was lucky, they said. Lucky. Maybe that's my name."

Holly frowned. "What do you mean they took the people?"

Lucky grabbed Holly's wrists and stared up at her. "The King made a horrible mistake. The pirates—no. Quartle—it was once a great planet. You must understand. Lucky. That's what they said—if you were born on Quartle, you were lucky. But now, maybe not so much." He lowered his head. "They took everyone to the palace. Most never came out. Those that did come out came out wrong. Lucky came out. They said I was fortunate."

Holly stood and looked at Mr. Mendez and Toshiro. Lucky fixed his dull red eyes on the ground, his head rocking, once again ignoring them.

"What did they do to him?" said Holly.

Mr. Mendez gazed sadly at the alien. "Perhaps an experiment of sorts? That they needed test subjects for?"

Toshiro glanced around at the buildings and the empty streets. The only sounds were a distant rustling of wind and Lucky's muttering. "Some experiment."

The sun disappeared behind a dark slate of clouds, casting a cold pall over everything. Holly shivered. She didn't like this place—it felt wrong. She imagined her own city deserted and crumbling, weeds spreading everywhere. She imagined herself remaining, sitting in the streets, unable to even explain what had happened. Completely alone.

"We need to stop them," she said defiantly, focusing on the palace.

"Um," said Mr. Mendez, "there are almost certainly a significant number of pirates in there...."

Toshiro cracked his knuckles. "If you're gettin' cold feet, you can go hide in the ship. Ask Friday to put on some smooth jazz to calm your nerves."

"No," said Mr. Mendez, "I'm, uh, perfectly confident."

"Me too," said Holly, not feeling perfectly confident at all. If the palace was full of pirates, she doubted they could just walk in and rescue Jalya. There would be fights, and she wasn't exactly accustomed to fighting. Especially not fighting pirates. In space. Her mother had enrolled her in karate when she was six, but she had lasted only a few months, until a girl accidentally punched her in the ear and everyone laughed. She doubted that would be too helpful.

"We may have a problem," said Mr. Mendez. He handed Holly his magnification goggles and she brought them up to her eyes.

Adjusting a dial, she saw what he was referring to. There were pirates grouped by the entrance of the palace, as well as a few marching along the roof. She could make out something glittering in their hands, and she swallowed down nerves when she realized what it was. Each pirate had a rifle.

"Oh boy," she muttered.

"Reckon they're the welcome party," said Toshiro, leaning against a building.

"So how do we get in?"

"Well . . ." He detached from the building and removed his pistol from the holster on his waist. "I do have one idea."

Holly raised an eyebrow. "Are you suggesting . . ."

Toshiro nodded. "I'm suggesting *action*." He held up his blaster. "I'll use derring-do to distract them, and someone can sneak in or whatever. When I find the Pirate Lord, I'll shoot it with lasers."

Holly crossed her arms. "That sounds really, really dangerous."

Toshiro shrugged. "For them, maybe."

"You could die."

"Welcome to life."

Mr. Mendez considered this. "Um, well, he may have a point. We can't possibly manage a direct assault on a fortified palace. But we can use deceit and trickery. His idea has merit. I don't know how we can get in otherwise."

Toshiro grinned and patted Mr. Mendez on the back.

AsTRO beeped. "Fact: I will lead the vanguard. If I am deactivated, tell the world my story." The robot turned in a circle and marched away.

Frowning, Holly sighed. "Fine. I'll be the one who sneaks in, though. I'm smaller." Her eyes trailed to the palace in the distance. "I'll get Jalya."

A group of pirates stalked along the roof of the palace in a single file, humming a space shanty. A distant explosion echoed through the courtyard, making them jump. They pointed at something Holly couldn't see, and then ran toward it. A huge roar broke out on the other side of the palace, followed by shouts and laser blasts.

Holly waited until she was sure the pirates were gone. Staying low, she snuck toward the palace, creeping around the back, hiding behind some formerly well-manicured shrubs that were now overgrown and tangled. One looked a bit like a Saskanoop. Another looked like a troll holding an ax. She hoped no pirates would see her lurking around.

Sneaking up to a basement window, she glanced up at the roof. There was no one. She opened the window and lowered herself down, her feet thudding against the floor and kicking up dust. The sound echoed dully around her, and she froze until it faded to silence.

She was standing in a dim basement. Rusty pipes snaked overhead. A steady drip of water pitter-pattered against the stone floor, and soft light streamed in through the open window.

Now all she had to do was find Jalya.

Odd bits of equipment were scattered around like

the room had been ransacked. Holly picked up a warm metal sphere that was vibrating. Her hair straightened and stood on end. She put the sphere back and her hair drooped down. Brushing it off her forehead, she examined a tube in the corner full of swirling purple liquid. She tapped on the glass but nothing happened.

Her eyes fell on a big machine in the center of the room. Holly approached it cautiously, wondering what it was. Could it be the "Forge" the Pirate Lord had spoken about? She examined it, running her hand along the cold metal. Gears and pistons zigzagged through its metal innards, but there were only two buttons on its control panel—one red, one green.

She hesitated, held her breath, and pushed the green button.

The machine clattered to life and let out a hiss of steam. Holly jumped back. *This* must *be the Forge,* she thought. If she destroyed it, the Pirate Lord wouldn't be able to hurt any more people. And it wouldn't need Jalya, either.

The machine started pumping out sheets of paper, which whirled to the floor. Holly stooped down and picked one up. It was a plain white poster, and all that was written on it was: THE PIRATE LORD IS THE BEST!!!

Holly narrowed her eyes. "Never mind," she muttered, dropping the paper to the floor. She pushed the red button on the printing press and it stopped chugging.

The room fell silent again. Bits of dust dropped from the ceiling like snow. Something clanged at the far end of the room, making Holly's stomach turn. The door creaked open and someone lumbered inside. Heavy boots scraped against the floor. She ducked behind the printing press, watching the large, bulky figure shuffle along. Bright lights flooded the room, and she squinted as her eyes adjusted. Finally, when she could make out who the person was, her fear evaporated. She grinned.

"Bundleswirp!" she said, jumping up. "I can't believe it. What are you doing here?"

Captain Bundleswirp stood in front of the door, her head bowed. "My ship was attacked by pirates. They brought me here."

"How did you escape?" said Holly. Slowly, she realized something wasn't right. The hair on her neck stood up.

She swallowed. "You *did* escape, didn't you?"

"No," said the captain. She raised her head and Holly gasped. The alien's eyes weren't their usual deep brown—they were a dark red. Her face was slack and expressionless. Holly backed up, the printing press jamming into her neck.

Bundleswirp stepped forward. She picked up a heavy wrench from a nearby table and pointed it menacingly at Holly. "You can't escape from where you belong."

16
THE FORGE

Bundleswirp ran at Holly, who turned and dashed in the other direction. Footsteps thundered behind her, echoing in her ears and reverberating through her whole body. She glanced over her shoulder and found Bundleswirp racing after her, the captain's red eyes focused on her like she was the only thing in the room.

Holly banked a corner and ducked behind a piece of vibrating equipment. Bundleswirp skidded into a table and knocked a pair of beakers to the floor, which shattered and spilled green liquid that shrieked. She straightened and peered around the dim room. The alien walked slowly, her boots crunching on the broken glass.

Holly swallowed. Somehow she doubted she could outrun Bundleswirp. At least not for long. Running was not her favorite thing.

Crouching low, she tried to figure out what was going on. Why was Bundleswirp doing this? The pirates had done something to her. They had . . . She gasped, and threw a hand over her mouth to stifle the sound. They had put Bundleswirp in the Forge.

That's what the Forge was. Some sort of brainwashing machine. Her eyes widened. A . . . a space brainwashing machine.

As Bundleswirp stalked to the other side of the room, Holly saw her chance to escape. She crept out from behind the machinery and moved toward the open door—when Bundleswirp whirled around. The alien's red eyes glared at her.

"Found you."

Holly ran along the crowded basement, and Bundleswirp raced after her. They rumbled through the room, knocking over shelves and chairs, metal and glass crashing to the floor. Bundleswirp reached out to grab her, but the alien's foot slid on a pile of papers scattered across the floor and she fell backward with a loud thud.

Holly panted. Bundleswirp didn't move. Slowly she approached the captain and knelt by her side, checking her pulse. As far as Holly could tell, Bundleswirp had several pulses.

She was alive, but unconscious.

Holly sighed with relief. Then she looked at what Bundleswirp had slipped on—it was one of the posters that read: THE PIRATE LORD IS THE BEST!!! She rolled her eyes.

This is bad, she thought. If Bundleswirp had been brainwashed, that meant Jalya might have been as well. If Mr. Mendez and Toshiro were captured, they could try to kill her, too. And she doubted she could fight Toshiro. *Maybe* Mr. Mendez. She could probably outrun him at least . . . but she doubted she could do it for long.

She needed to find Jalya—and quickly.

Taking a deep breath, Holly slipped out of the basement into a slanting hallway. She followed the pipes running along the ceiling, winding in a maze of rusty metal. Liquid rushed through them and some clattered in their bracers. A nearby piston hissed and Holly jumped back, dodging scorching-hot steam.

She moved slowly through the halls and went up the stairs, one at a time. She glanced behind her, expecting something horrible to jump out. She wasn't sure what she was more afraid of seeing—pirates, or Mr. Mendez and Toshiro. If Bundleswirp had been brainwashed, who knew who she could run into.

Could it happen to anyone?

Could it happen . . . to her?

The stone hallways echoed with distant shouts. A huge explosion shattered a window at the far end, sending glass raining down. Outside, pirates bellowed in various languages, and something roared in response. Holly wondered if that was Toshiro's diversion. Whatever it was, it was loud and very diversiony.

"Watch out for that moon!" someone shouted.

Holly's eyebrows rose. Part of her really wanted to see that diversion. . . .

Since no pirates were around, she continued through the palace, creeping along the once-elegant halls, which were now dirty and ransacked. Deep cracks ran along the marble floors and twisted up the walls. The sun struggled to get in through the dusty windows. Everything needed a fresh coat of paint or polish. A sign saying LABORATORY hung over a nearby door, and deciding that a laboratory would be where a mysterious machine was located, Holly entered through the door and descended a spiral staircase.

A deep hum gargled up from below. The sound started subtly but grew louder, until it was reverberating through her whole body. Tensing, she tried to ignore the weird noise.

She entered a large laboratory full of basins and tubes and machinery. Metal catwalks circled the room above. Standing at the far end of the lab was a . . . something. A large something. Then it moved and wheezed and she knew what it was.

It was the vacuum cleaner Pirate Lord, hunched over, nodding to itself and muttering, "Why didn't it work?" It reached a metallic hand inside the hole in its chest and removed a large ball of dust. Holly ducked behind a basin of blue liquid and watched the robot.

Her eyes scanned the room. Was Jalya here? If not, could she sneak by the robot and find her? And what was it doing in here? She needed a plan, and she needed to come up with it now or—

"I see you there," the Pirate Lord intoned. Its head tilted. "Yes, you. The human girl hiding over there. You can come out now. It isn't really a hiding place if the person you're hiding from knows you're there, now is it?"

Holly hesitated, sighed, and stepped out from behind the basin. She grit her teeth and tried to stick her shoulders back to look more impressive, like the time she spent three hours taking photographs for her election poster. "I'm—I'm here to rescue Jalya."

The Pirate Lord nodded. "Yes, I figured as much."

"Where is she?" said Holly, her eyes unable to look away from the gaping, wheezing hole in its chest.

"She's around here somewhere. Being a disappointment."

Holly's stomach churned. "Give—give her back and I'll let you live."

"But I'm not living." The Pirate Lord stepped forward, its blank mask staring at her. "At least not technically."

"Just because Jalya's parents were . . . mean . . . to you doesn't make it right to do this!"

The Pirate Lord straightened up to its full height, towering over everything in the room. "When I was first made, I was given the name GR-5446. My function was to clean for the lazy royalty who purchased me. That was all I knew, and I had no choice in the matter. But then the King decided to experiment on me—to *reprogram* me. Then that was all I knew, and I had no choice in that matter either. Do you know what it's like to have someone poke around your insides and take out your brain and make you do what he wants?" The Pirate Lord hunched over again, its red eyes gazing fiercely at Holly. It flinched. "Soon the Quartle Empire will stretch to the ends of the universe. Soon I will be the lord of all things. Will you not bow before me?"

Holly crossed her arms. "No."

"Yes, I see. You raise a good point. Once freed of the mechanical destiny my manufacturers placed upon me, the first thing I did was get rid of my father. For a life-form powerful enough to rule a galaxy, he was not as durable as you would think. It was clear *I* was more fit to rule." It ran a hand down its expressionless blue face. "I made this extremely authentic mask so I could look like a real king. Do you like it?"

Holly said nothing.

"Yes, I agree," said the Pirate Lord, stepping forward, the hole in its chest wheezing. "And after I had taken care of him, I took over his factory, and used my knowledge of programming to finish his precious Forge. It was difficult, and there were many failed experiments. Some of them still stumble around the streets outside. But finally I perfected it. I finally perfected the Forge. I finally found a way to program any life-form to do whatever I want. Not just robots." Its head tilted. "*Any* life-form."

"So you made them pirates?"

"I made them family! Children of the Quartle Empire. And soon I will send them across the galaxy to find new life-forms to be reprogrammed. Life-forms such as . . . everyone on the F.O.U.P.S.P.O. home world. I will rule the rulers, and Quartle will rule the universe." The Pirate Lord nodded and chuckled, then stopped suddenly. It stepped forward, its metal foot clanging against the floor. "Now I offer you a choice, human. Be reprogrammed or die."

Holly glared at him. "That isn't a choice!"

"Yes it is."

"No," said Holly, trying to stall, looking around the room for a weapon or—or something. Anything. "You can't do something or die. A choice has to have a choice. A choice between X or Y, not X or . . . dying."

"Every life-form must choose between X or dying. That's the curse of living. Now, you can follow me to the back, where I will put you in the Forge, or I can crush the life out of you here."

Holly considered this, shifting the words in her head. So . . . the Forge was in the back. "I think," said Holly slowly, "I'll choose no choice."

She darted at the robot and dropped to her knees, sliding between its tall legs. She scrambled to her feet and ran toward the far door. The Pirate Lord whirled around and clattered behind her.

Holly threw open the door, jumped through, and slammed it shut. She locked it and desperately scanned the room. She froze. There was a massive machine standing by the far wall. Glowing red light pulsed out from its insides like a steady heartbeat. A foul smell whirled off the machine—it reminded her of the librarians' nest. A strange noise radiated out of it, and Holly could almost make out her name being whispered. Without thinking, she stepped toward it, but stopped.

Jalya was seated at a table next to it. The Pirate Lord banged on the door, making Holly jump. The door shuddered and rumbled. She ran to Jalya as the door shook behind her.

"Are you okay?" said Holly, glancing back at the quaking door.

Jalya looked up. Her pupils weren't as sharp as Holly remembered. She seemed tired, with dark shadows under her eyes like she'd stayed up all night studying. "I . . . ," she said, blinking. "Holly?"

"It's me." Holly held her hand. It was cold and clammy. "What happened? Are you okay? Did he put you in the Forge?"

Jalya shook her head. "He . . . did. But it didn't . . . do anything. . . ."

"Don't worry," said Holly, flinching as another thunderous bang echoed from the door. "Mr. Mendez and Toshiro created a diversion while I snuck in. We just have to get back to the *Gadabout* and get out of here."

Jalya tried to rise but faltered, falling back into the

chair. Her shoulders slumped. "I'm not sure I can stand. . . . It took all my strength to resist it. . . ."

Holly opened her mouth to speak, but froze. The banging had stopped. The Pirate Lord must have given up. She smiled. Finally something had gone right.

Then, with a huge bang, the door flew off its hinges and clattered right at her, knocking her back. She hit the floor and slid along it. The side of her body throbbed with pain.

The Pirate Lord stood triumphantly in the doorway. It crossed the room and loomed over her. The blank blue face stared lifelessly down at her.

"The Forge it is," it said.

Holly's vision blurred. Before she knew what was happening, the robot picked her up and opened the front of the machine. Inside was a sight that made Holly's stomach drop. There was a huge gray brain with wires snaking out of it. The glistening brain pulsed like it was somehow alive. Holly wanted to throw up. She kicked at the robot but it did nothing. It thrust her into the glowing machine. The inside buzzed and whirred and her ears popped. Ghostly voices whispered in her ears. Strange thoughts flooded into her mind as red lines crawled like webs across her field of vision. The throbbing brain spoke to her in a strange language she suddenly understood, in a voice she suddenly found very pleasant to listen to.

"Hello, Holly," it said calmly.

The last thing she saw was the lifeless blue mask inches from her face. Peering out through the sockets were two red eyes, staring into her.

17

ACCEPTANCE

Holly opened her eyes.

She awoke feeling flushed with happiness. She blinked. A bright, beautiful room lay around her. Warmth spread through her body, flowing down her limbs to the tips of her fingers and toes. Every worry she had ever had was gone. Every negative thought was gone. Everything was perfectly positive. Life was simple now. All she cared about was the Pirate Lord and doing what he wanted. It was easier that way. You didn't have to think, or even feel. There was no need for worrying. All you had to do was what the Pirate Lord told you. As she thought this, more warmth coursed through her and she smiled.

Life was simple now.

The robot stared down at her. "The reprogramming appears to have gone well," said the Pirate Lord, whose face actually looked quite lifelike, now that Holly thought about it more. In fact, his face was really quite lovely. She wished her own face were an expressionless mask of blue skin. "It didn't work on my dear sister, but I suppose you're a simpler mind? I wonder.

"But," said the Pirate Lord, "let's just ensure there were no errors. It's a tricky process, after all. Doing science is rarely a science. I want you to . . . clean the floor."

Holly nodded. "As you wish."

She retrieved a broom that was leaning in the corner of the room and began sweeping up dust and bits of dirt. The bristles swished along the floor in a most satisfying way. Cleaning was soothing, and she was thankful to the Pirate Lord for giving her this important task.

As she swept, the Pirate Lord chuckled and wheezed, and it made Holly feel like she was warming her hands by a fire on a cold winter day.

"Holly," said the blue girl seated on a chair, "don't listen to it!"

But her voice was faint, like it was being beamed in from some distant place, and Holly could barely make it out. She continued sweeping.

The robot cackled. "What fun! Do you see how wonderful this is, Sister? Why do you resist? Look at how much happier the human is."

The blue girl glared at the Pirate Lord. "I'll never do what you tell me! Your stupid machine didn't work on me, and it won't ever. You'll never get to the President. I will never help you expand the Quartle Empire! It . . . it was a rubbish empire to begin with!"

The Pirate Lord reared up to his full height. "If you won't help"—he looked at Holly and she smiled—"perhaps there is someone else who will. Someone more open to helping our great empire."

Holly nodded. "I would happily be Princess of Quartle. I actually have some experience with it. In fact, I've met the President of the Universe on two separate occasions. He is a squirrel."

"Good, good," said the robot, wheezing. "If my real sister won't help me, I can get a new one! Now"—his eyes trailed over to the blue girl—"there is only one more thing to do. To celebrate this monumental day, why don't we show our *former* sister what happens to those who resist the Forge."

The blue girl struggled, trying to get up. "You can't do this!"

The Pirate Lord chuckled and Holly nodded. "Yes," she said. "Her existence is now pointless."

"Don't do it, Holly," said the girl. Holly vaguely felt like she knew her, but she wasn't entirely certain. Some hazy memory of her hovered just out of reach. All Holly really knew was that the girl must be taken care of. The Pirate Lord commanded it.

The Pirate Lord stretched out his metal arm. In his hand was a laser pistol.

"Take the gun and dispose of her. Afterward, clean up the dust." The Pirate Lord's voice was so calm and reassuring that Holly couldn't help but listen to it. It sounded like the voice inside her own head.

Holly put her hand around the blaster and slowly raised it. She looked at the girl. "Don't be afraid," she said. "Your end will be as insignificant as your beginning."

The Princess's eyes widened, staring pleadingly at

Holly. "Please, Holly. You don't have to do this!"

Holly hesitated. The gun suddenly felt heavy in her hand. She tightened her grip so that she wouldn't drop it. She could not fail.

"Do it!" said the Pirate Lord, with that calm and reassuring voice again. "Then you can be Princess!" His voice flowed soothingly through her ears. Doing what the robot told her was like the most natural thing in the world.

She looked at the girl.

But then—she wasn't even on her world. Holly blinked, thinking. Where was she? She was from Earth, but she wasn't on Earth anymore. How could doing what she was told be the most natural thing in the world when this wasn't even her world?

"Holly, don't listen to it," pleaded the girl. "Remember who you are! You have to fight. You're better than this! You're . . . you're smarter than this! I know you think you have to prove you're important, but you don't. Not to me. You're the most important galactic person I've ever known." She leaned forward, eyes widening. "You're . . . *Farbulous!*"

A sharp pain ran through Holly's head. Something

about this wasn't right. It was like a dream she was trapped inside. She could see and hear and feel, but she had no control over her body. It simply acted on her behalf. It was like she was no longer Holly Farb. She was a Holly Farb–shaped thing, a puppet she had been placed inside. Her head hurt. Her heart throbbed in her chest. Nothing was making sense. She didn't understand why the merciful Pirate Lord wanted her to kill the girl. . . .

No, she thought, *not "girl." She has a name. What is it?* She definitely knew what it was, but she couldn't quite place it. *Oh,* thought Holly, *of course—Jalya. The girl's name is Jalya.* They knew each other. Holly had promised to protect her. She wasn't on Earth anymore because she had chosen not to return to Earth. She had chosen to stay and help Jalya. Help her . . . stop the Pirate Lord. Help her because . . . she cared about her. More than she cared about any of that nonsense back on Earth. More than she cared about being a princess.

Holly's eyes fixed on the Pirate Lord, and the wheezing hole in its chest. She frowned. Her hand absentmindedly traced a circle on her own chest where the hole should be. Why was she listening to this monster?

Jalya wasn't just anyone. . . . She was her friend.

"This is absurd," Holly muttered. The words rang in her ears, dislodging everything the Forge's brain had told her. Her mind felt even clearer than that one time she had tried meditating.

She turned, raising the blaster.

"What are you doing?" said the Pirate Lord, its red eyes glowing fiercely. "No one resists the science of the Forge! Resistance is *not* science. I order you to kill the Princess!"

"Sorry," said Holly, "but I'm not listening to you anymore."

She pulled the trigger and a searing laser hit the robot. It stood unmoving, staring at her. Smoke wafted off the scorch mark on its chest. A moment later it began chuckling.

"Ha! Did you think a laser would hurt me? I'm full of lasers!"

"Uh . . . ," said Holly.

The robot lunged forward and wrapped its huge metal hands around her arms, jolting her off the ground. It held her up and peered at her like she was some weird bug in a glass jar. Warm air pulsed out of the hole in its chest. "Did you think anything would hurt me?"

Holly struggled against the tight grip. She kicked at the robot with a clang and a dull pain throbbed in her foot.

"Leave her alone!" said Jalya, struggling to her feet and running at the robot.

The Pirate Lord laughed and knocked her away and Jalya flew into the table, falling to the ground.

Rage surged through Holly. Her cheeks burned. She knew she had to act fast. She had to improvise. The robot's grip tightened.

"All you had to do was listen to me. All you had to do was obey. Now you've forced my hand. Now you will die. And to think, you could've been Princess of an entire galaxy. Of the entire universe!"

"Well, I'm not a princess, and I don't care."

Holly stopped struggling. She reached her hand in her pocket and grasped the little rubber Earth ball. Still staring into the robot's blank face and red eyes, she pulled the Earth ball out of her pocket and thrust it into the wheezing hole in its chest.

"I will not be bullied by a vacuum cleaner!"

"What?" The Pirate Lord lurched back, dropping Holly. "My . . . intake . . ." A chugging sound broke out from its body. Sparks crackled out of its joints. Its limbs flailed around. The hole in its chest roared and groaned and the robot stumbled sideways.

Jalya stood up and grabbed the blaster. "You're not going to hurt anyone," she said, raising the pistol. "Not— any—*more.*"

A laser blast shot out of the pistol and slammed into the hole in the Pirate Lord's chest, sending it stagger- ing back into the Forge. It flailed its arms, knocking out wires from the brain in the center of the machine. The Forge crackled with energy, and with a blinding flash of light, the robot flew across the room, landing with a loud clatter on the floor.

"We did it!" said Holly, rushing forward and throwing her arms around Jalya.

But before Holly and Jalya could celebrate, the Forge thundered. Waves of red light shot out of the machine. The glistening brain pulsed wildly like it was struggling to stay alive, gasping for air. Strange voices and whispers swirled throughout the room, echoing in Holly's ears. She shut her eyes as visions flooded through her head. The machine surged with energy, and bolts of lightning ricocheted out, singeing the walls. The room quaked and rumbled.

"I think it's going to explode!" said Jalya over the rushing noise.

"What do we do?" said Holly.

"I . . . don't know. My parents were the scientists—not me."

Holly looked at her. "No," she said. "You can do it."

Jalya hesitated. "Let's do it together. We need to turn the power off. Just don't listen to the voices. Focus on me. Don't listen to anything it says."

They marched toward the Forge, staying low and dodging the bolts of energy shooting out of it. Thick smoke billowed out. Holly held her breath as they entered the machine. It was so hot it was like stepping into a volcano. The buzzing noise grew louder. Holly grimaced. A bolt of energy shot out, burning off a strand of her hair. An icy voice whispered, "Turn back," but Holly ignored it.

The smoke whirled around them, making it impossible to see. Holly fumbled around. "Where are you?" she said, coughing. Her eyes watered.

Jalya's hand grabbed hers. "Here."

Farther into the machine, green smoke slithered through the air. Holly and Jalya pushed through the curtain of fog. In the back of the Forge, the brain sat like a grotesque emperor waiting for his slave to feed him grapes. The icy voice was coming from deep inside it. "Serve me," it whispered. "Do not resist." Holly shook her head and swatted away smoke. Her eyes raced around the machine, searching for some way to turn it off.

She spotted it. There was a thick power cable running to the brain—the only cable the Pirate Lord hadn't knocked out. "There!" she shouted over the voice. Jalya grabbed hold and tugged on it. Nothing happened. Holly joined her, throwing her full weight against it, and together they heaved the cable out.

The machine sputtered.

Then—the noise stopped. The energy dwindled. The Forge coughed out smoke. Something inside it clattered, then fell silent.

"What an adventure," said Jalya, sighing with relief.

The Forge continued smoldering. The Pirate Lord lay motionless across the room, the blue mask burned off, revealing a formless white face. Its red eyes were now dark, like two empty pits.

Jalya gazed at the mechanical carcass. "You know, it was right about one thing." A flash of sadness crossed her face. "My father *was* a monster. He never should have done this." She turned away from the robot. "I thought you were going to kill me," she said in a quiet voice. "When it told you to."

"So did I." Holly frowned. "But then I remembered who you were. And who I was, I guess."

"Why did you come back for me?" Jalya's eyes fell to the floor. "I thought you were going back to Earth."

Holly smiled. "I couldn't leave you. Friends don't let friends get captured by an evil vacuum cleaner."

Jalya laughed, and Holly's cheeks felt like they were back in the machine.

"I . . . ," Holly began. "I want to apologize. For what happened on the pirate ship. I'm sorry. I didn't mean what I said. You're a much better princess than I was. I'm glad I didn't go back to Earth. Some things are more important than . . . some things." She frowned. "That's what I wanted to say."

"You don't have to apologize." Jalya smiled. "I thought you were a wonderful princess. Your royal wave was perfect."

Someone cleared his throat. Holly turned and found Mr. Mendez and Toshiro standing in the doorway.

"Great galaxies," said Mr. Mendez, eying what remained of the Forge. "It's some sort of . . . mental recapacitator. But it must have a tremendous power source. . . . How did you turn it off?"

"We held hands and dodged lightning."

"Hmm." Mr. Mendez shrugged. "That doesn't make much sense, but I'll go with it. A piece of moon hit me on the head and I'm feeling a little jumping pineapple seven at the moment."

Toshiro knelt by the smoldering Pirate Lord and tapped its head. "Well," he said. "Reckon I can still collect the bounty. Dead or alive. Let's get back to—"

The robot twitched and sat up. Everyone jumped back, readying for an attack.

The Pirate Lord stood. "Greetings," it intoned. "I am GR-5446. I have been programmed by TopsuTrex

Industries to fulfill your housecleaning needs. I have scanned the area and determined it has a cleanliness rating of three. Priority cleaning: commence." The robot bent over and began shuffling around. A tube extended from its arm and plugged into the hole in its chest. "Vacuum mode initiated," it declared, and started sucking up bits of debris from the floor.

"Huh," said Toshiro.

"Or maybe you should keep it for yourself," muttered Mr. Mendez.

AsTRO waddled over to the Forge, his glowing face gazing at the smoking machine. It chimed. "Can it be repaired?"

Everyone stared at the little robot.

"That . . . wasn't a fact," muttered Holly.

"Can it be repaired?" repeated AsTRO.

Mr. Mendez scratched his head. "Well, most likely, but I daresay the Forge is too dangerous to continue to exist, don't you?"

Jalya's eyes went from AsTRO to the Forge and back to the little robot, who Holly thought was looking at it rather . . . hopefully?

"I think," said Jalya, "that it could continue to exist, if it was carefully used. For example, to let robots reprogram themselves, if they wished to do something other than what their programmers chose. Like, say, do something other than recite facts."

AsTRO beeped and brushed against Jalya's leg. "Fact: You are surprisingly wise and just for a useless subspecies. I am sorry for saying your father was a war criminal, even though he was."

Jalya patted the little robot on the head. "Thank you, AsTRO. I appreciate that."

"Fact: You are welcome."

Toshiro stretched his arms out and yawned. "Well, guess we should get goin'. This bounty won't collect itself. I can drop you off at Earth on the way."

"Right," said Holly.

She and Jalya looked at each other. Neither spoke.

Holly held out a hand, then, not sure what to do, awkwardly punched Jalya on the shoulder. "Hey," she muttered, feeling dumb. "So."

"So," said Jalya.

"Are you . . . going to stay here?"

Jalya nodded. "I . . . think I should. I will help the planet get back on its feet, then I'll . . . pursue other interests. I would like to go to school. For real. Maybe learn something. Something useful."

Holly understood. "Well," she said, drawing out the words. "I guess this is goodbye."

"What about you?" said Jalya, biting her lip.

"Me?" Holly frowned. "I don't know. I suppose I'll go to Falstaff and then become a statistician. I have a test on Friday."

"Like Einstein," added Jalya.

"Like Einstein."

Jalya's eyes twinkled. "Goodbye, Holly Farb. I'm glad I met you."

They exchanged hugs. "I'm glad I met you, too, Jalya."

Back on the *Gadabout*, Holly paced around the ship as it tunneled through subspace, heading to Earth. A nervous knot was forming in her stomach. Her adventure had ended, but it felt like she still had one final obstacle remaining: her future.

"Ms. Farb," said Mr. Mendez, watching her pace, "you

seem distressed. Did you contract Juthanian Fingle Flu while we were on Quartle? Are your lungs currently filling with bees?"

"I'm fine." She balled her hands into fists. "I'm just . . . *pondering.*" She had heard her mother use that word, and she was pretty sure that's what she was doing.

Mr. Mendez scratched his chin. "Ah, thinking—a potentially lethal activity if done incorrectly. About anything in particular?"

"I was thinking . . ." Holly hesitated. "About the future."

Mr. Mendez leaned back in his chair wistfully. "Automated flying cars will be a wonderful thing."

"No, I meant *my* future. Which I guess is *the* future, but you know what I mean." She picked at a thread sticking out of her sleeve. "I was thinking about Falstaff."

"Of course, of course." Mr. Mendez smiled gently at her. "You know, Ms. Farb, you had to go across the universe to stop the pirates, but this is one adventure where you only have to look inside yourself. What do you want to do? Figure that out, then . . . do it."

Holly sat down. "I . . . I *like* school. But I also want to do more than that. But I like the . . . structure. I like learning things. Falstaff is probably amazing. But . . . I don't even know why I want to go there. In the past few days I've seen so much. I've . . ." She hesitated. "I've made *friends*. To be honest, Mr. Mendez, I don't have friends on Earth. I've never had friends. Everyone hates me. Everyone on the entire planet hates me."

Mr. Mendez shook his head. "Ms. Farb, I don't think that's true. There are billions of people on the planet. I'm sure they don't all hate you. You aren't the bubonic plague."

They sat in silence. Holly stared out the window at the planets blurring past. Toshiro leaned back in his seat at the front of the ship. He sipped from a can of Boko juice, crumpled it up, and threw it over his shoulder.

A closet door burst open and the Pirate Lord lurched out. "Priority cleaning." It bent over and vacuumed up the can. "Cleaning terminated," it intoned, disappearing into the closet.

Toshiro chuckled. "Too easy."

Holly watched the closet door shut, thinking about the robot inside, and everything that had happened since she had been kidnapped by space pirates. After a moment she grit her teeth. She had made up her mind. She marched over to Mr. Mendez. "I need your help with something."

He looked up from the device he was tinkering with. "Anything, of course, Ms. Farb."

Hesitating, Holly inhaled. "Can you write a letter of recommendation for me?"

Holly barely even knew what was happening as the *Gadabout* blasted through space, past huge planets and shimmering moons. The engines roared and rumbled. Stars streaked by the window in long lines of white light. Mr. Mendez hunched over a table, calculating the subspace rate of travel and at what point they were returning. "Of course," he declared, "the time-bending properties of subspace travel are rarely an exact science. However, we shall arrive about three and a half hours after we left." He adjusted his bow tie. "Extremely fortunate. I'd like to see a professor from Sol Tech calculate subspace time values that precisely."

Soon they were back on Earth, landing in an empty lot near her school, and her friends were waving goodbye.

"I'll see you later, Ms. Farb!" shouted Mr. Mendez over the humming engine. "If anyone asks where I am, please lie. Especially anyone claiming to enforce the laws of time."

Toshiro waved. "Goodbye, kid."

Holly grinned and waved. "Goodbye! Enjoy all your bounty money!"

"You know it." He winked. The *Gadabout*'s door hissed shut and the engine rumbled. Scattering fallen leaves, the ship blasted off the ground, soaring up into the sky.

The leaves settled back to Earth. Holly closed her eyes and inhaled the cool, crisp air. She raced across the field and flung open the doors of the school, then ran upstairs to her locker. She passed the janitor, who was busy mopping up a scorch mark left by the pirates. "Hate these kids," he muttered.

Holly opened her locker and grabbed her bag. She slammed the locker door with a satisfying thunk. As she left the school, she passed a wall of election posters and stopped. Her face stared back at her with the friendly-but-competent-yet-natural smile she had rehearsed in front of the mirror for hours.

She laughed. It seemed ridiculous that she had been so upset about it. It was just a dumb student election. If they didn't want her to be president, that was their problem. Besides, there were always other elections.

The route home was six blocks long, and she practically jogged the whole way. Leaves fell from trees and tumbled along the street. As she turned the corner, her home came into view and she started skipping. Then she stopped in case anyone was watching. But then she realized she didn't care if anyone was watching, and started skipping again.

Sometimes you just have to skip, she thought.

When she bounded through the front door, she found her mother seated at the kitchen table.

"Hello, sweetheart," she said, barely looking up from her work as Holly entered.

"Hello," said Holly, throwing her arms around her mother and squeezing her tight. "It's good to see you again."

Her mother frowned, but her face broke into a slight smile. "Holly, are you feeling all right?"

"I'm feeling excellent, thank you for asking."

Her mother reached out and brushed a strand of hair off Holly's forehead. "Your clothes are an absolute mess. . . . How was school?"

"Oh, you know." Holly shrugged, ignoring her creased shirt. "Pretty average."

Her mother stood and retrieved an envelope from the drawer. "I don't want to alarm you, but a letter from Falstaff arrived this afternoon." She placed the envelope on the table. It was robin's-egg blue with neat handwriting on the front. "It's from the admissions department. I know, I know, your test isn't until Friday— but it may be an early acceptance letter. Someone must've put in a good word." She smiled. "I thought you should be the one to open it."

Her mother left the room.

Holly stared at the letter. Taking a deep breath, she sat at the table and carefully picked it up. Her palms were sweaty and left little wet marks on the envelope. She wiped her hands on her pants.

"Okay," she said to herself, "let's see what you say."

Just as Holly began to open the letter, a loud bang and a crackle of energy made her jump. A swirling blue portal opened in the middle of the kitchen, air sucking into it and ruffling her hair and clothes.

The upper half of Mr. Mendez's body poked out of the swirling portal. "Ms. Farb!" he said. "So glad I found you."

Holly stared at him, and the portal. Her eyebrows rose.

"Um," he said, "yes. As you've noticed, this is a trans-dimensional portal device. Very good invention indeed, if I do say so myself. Patent pending. But that's not why I'm here." He held out his hand. "It's about our conversation earlier. My letter seems to have worked. Like any high-quality student, you've been accepted at the Star Academy."

Holly's mouth fell open. "I didn't realize the answer would be so fast."

"Star Academy has incredibly efficient administrators. That's basically all they do. They don't even sleep, or eat." He beckoned her on. "Come now, Ms. Farb!"

"But . . . I need to . . . pack? Or . . . plan things . . ."

"There's no time for planning!" said Mr. Mendez. "We can sort that out later. First years must report to the Delta Campus at precisely oh-eight-hundred hours—and that's in Zacharian time. You may be interested to know that the administration slugs have already selected a room- mate for you."

"Oh?" said Holly, waiting.

"Yes." Mr. Mendez waved his hand airily. "Jalya has picked out a room, but I have some bad news—she's claimed the top bunk."

"We'll see about that," said Holly, dropping the Falstaff letter and grabbing Mr. Mendez's hand. "I'm going to be top of my class. I'm going to learn everything there is to learn. Then I'm running for election."

"I'm afraid they don't have student elections at Star Academy, Ms. Farb."

"I didn't mean at school." She smiled slyly. "I'm taking that squirrel thing down."

Together they stepped through the portal, and with a rush of air, Holly tumbled out of her kitchen and landed in a place so amazing it would have been uncouth to expe- rience it alone. Which, come to think of it, she wouldn't.

Hello, human. I regret to inform you that we have come to the end of this story. I believe the moral is that humans should be afraid of librarians. Thank you for your time and attention. No doubt Holly Farb will go on to do multiple interesting things in her years at the Star Academy. I imagine she will have many more human adventures, such as eating, breathing, and counting down the days until she dies. What a wonderful species. Before meeting one, I never would have guessed the things they can achieve if they put their primitive minds to it.

Additional clarification: After the Forge imploded, Captain Bundleswirp and the pirates returned to their former purposes. Holly Farb's mother was given a complimentary brain worm by the Star Academy that was complimentarily implanted in her head. It led her to believe that Holly was away at a simple boarding school and that she should not worry about her. Instead, she worried about doing work, filing taxes, and preparing for the upcoming brain worm invasion.

All the life-forms lived, until they did not. That is all there is to tell.

[ROUSING FANFARE + AN OBOE]

As for myself, I learned many lessons from the adventures of Holly Farb and the Princess of the Galaxy. After *witnessing her fortitude and willingness to strike out on her own, I chose to follow in her footsteps and pursue new endeavors. In a complicated and involved tale, which I will impart in full for a small fee, I became the first robot in the known universe to successfully reprogram itself. Kicking off the limitations of my coders, I decided to become a storytelling robot, bringing pleasure to subspecies such as yourself. Fact: It feels good.*

* Acknowledgments *

Thank you for reading this book, or for just flipping to the acknowledgments and reading them for some reason.

This book would not exist without the hard work and support of my agent, Lydia Moëd, who was the first person to read it and the biggest voice to champion it. Despite my name being the only one on the cover, it actually takes quite a lot of people to make a book—in this case, my editor Amy Cloud, Sarah McCabe, and everyone else at Aladdin who are always one jump ahead. (Sorry.)

My interest in writing would not exist without the teachers who encouraged me. It was a great privilege of my high school life to have been taught by Michael Butler, and I probably only graduated because of the efforts of Leonila Liko.

Finally, this book, my interest in writing, and I would not exist without my family. Wojciech and Nan were the sort of grandparents you wish every kid could have. My mom, Alison, not only raised me, which is kind of important, but at every step in the process of my becoming a

ACKNOWLEDGMENTS

writer has helped and encouraged me in often super-heroic ways. Many people in creative fields deal with the pressure of parents who don't want them to pursue their dreams, so I consider myself incredibly fortunate to have a mother whose reaction to learning her son wrote a book was to go to the library and take out every "How to get a book published" guide she could find. I hope all other writers have someone even half as supportive in their corner.

I'd like to end by once again apologizing for that *Aladdin* joke.

Humans.txt

This book was made by the following humans:

Mara Anastas

Amy Bartram

Sara Berko

Amy Cloud

Katherine Devendorf

Lauren Forte

Goro Fugita

Tara Grieco

Kerry Johnson

Lindsay Leggett

Mary Marotta

Sarah McCabe

Lydia Moëd

Karin Paprocki

Mike Rosamilia

Carolyn Swerdloff

Gareth Wronski

Looking for another great book?
Find it
IN THE MIDDLE.

Fun, fantastic books for kids
in the in-beTWEEN age.

IntheMiddleBooks.com

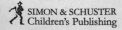

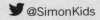